Dixieland Short Stories
of a Peculiar Nature

Bill Hunt

NOTICE

The stories in this book are fictitious, except where and if noted by the author. Names, characters, places, and incidents are the product of the author's imagination and are used fictitiously. Any resemblance to actual persons, living or dead, businesses, companies, or locales is entirely coincidental.

Copyright © 2013 Bill Hunt
All rights reserved.

ISBN: 1490423907
ISBN-13: 9781490423906

Library of Congress Control Number: 2013911317
CreateSpace Independent Publishing Platform
North Charleston, South Carolina

LOOK AWAY, LOOK AWAY INDEX

TEN SOMEWHAT PECULIAR STORIES

THE BROWNING	1
THE LAST DAFFODIL	37
SPECIAL ARRANGEMENTS AT MICKEY SPITZER'S	51
A GOOD SON	63
THE ENCHANTING DR. MARQUISE AND RHETT	87
HOW SCRAPPLE GOT INTO MOMMA'S KITCHEN	105
SOUL MATES	119
WILLIE	131
CHRISTMAS CAKES	159
THE LAST TIME I SAW PARIS	169

THE BROWNING

"You should know first, that times were stranger then, and for no reason at all, someone might kill you," she said, her voice breaking while her eyes darted from my face to my hands. I didn't want to show I was scared. She pressed her fist to her chest; her eyes wide open and set on my face. "He said my parents were killed in a race riot in New Orleans when I was a baby." Her head moved in denial. "And when I was eleven, he sent me away." Her jaws locked for a second, her chin rose, and her eyes became slits. Her lips quivered with anger, and as her eyebrows rose, deep groves cut across her forehead, and then her round eyes turned as black as her hair. "And when I was twenty-five, he just as well as *murdered me,* the son of a bitch!"

Miss Royals shouted those words straight at me before I had a chance to tell her my name. That was my first visit to The Wilderness, and I'd been ushered to the dining room, a big room, dark and shadowy, and made worse by an overcast sky. Her outburst shook me, and my face burned. I took a deep breath and waited, standing motionless in my new, well-creased khakis and the blue blazer I'd bought to impress her. I knew right then my well-rehearsed introduction was shot to hell. Her makeup, jewels, and hair reminded me of an old Barbie found in the bottom of an abandoned toy box, but among it all, I recognized that Miss Royals was once a beautiful woman. Anxious then, I considered apologizing and giving up the assignment and leaving, but at that moment, she spread a fan of black feathers, graciously moving it to hide her mouth and chin. "I am Miss Jesse Royals," she said ever so slowly in a soft voice, and then with squinting eyes locked on my face, she shook her head and asked: "And why in hell would they send a damn kid to write my story, and a Mexican at that?"

I sucked in a big breath of air and a nervous laugh came close to bursting out. The implications in her question, however, I'd felt before in other places and times, but now it no longer raised ire, and besides, I was proud of my heritage, both sides: a great soldier father with green eyes and light hair who hailed from the UK and a loving mother with a hearty Guatemalan, not Mexican, birthright, and whose hair and skin I'd inherited. At that moment, on our first visit, I figured it best to stand and take whatever Miss Royals might dish out, and hope that in a short time she'd get to know me, and maybe I'd learn who she truly was and why she'd turned into a venomous, angry old lady. I smiled and politely answered her question.

"I'm here because I'm the newest reporter on staff, and I wanted this assignment," I said softly. "Wanting the assignment" wasn't the whole truth, but I figured it might soften the anger that apparently had taken over her life. I smiled. But then, her feather fan moved in quick jerks, the same as her cold, strange eyes as they scanned me over and over.

Miss Royals was believed to be the richest woman in the state, and according to my editor, she had not been seen outside her mansion for over forty years, the mansion in the marshlands on an island near the ocean in South Louisiana. Few people had dared to venture onto the estate, and for years the servants who lived there took care of everything that made up "The Wilderness." Upon further inquiry, I learned that the lady's name was seldom heard anymore except from the bankers and lawyers who cared for her wealth or as a curiosity in the community. Sometimes she was the *star* ghost or the villain in a story contrived by someone who claimed to have seen her "once upon a time." And now, according to my editor and her lawyers with whom he'd dealt, Miss Royals had decided "to right the lies that had entertained the community for fifty years."

"Get the facts," my editor said, "and I want your best work for *Escape* in the Christmas edition."

Looking back to the day he gave me the assignment, I see now that there was something amiss about his approach, possibly his smirk and words that caused me to feel as though I were being set up. In all probability, he knew I'd be thrown like a piece of raw meat into a lion's den. And in the back of my mind at the time, I'd decided I was being checked out to determine my "worth" to the newspaper, but that in itself didn't bother me. Truly, I felt honored to write the lady's story and was determined to prove my writing skills to the local readers in a conservative, Deep South town five hundred miles from where I'd grown up—in the oilfields of south Texas. I was excited about the assignment and took it as a challenge, knowing that if it turned out well, its success could be a step for me into the world of journalistic writing.

When the day came for our first visit, Miss Royal's driver picked me up at the newspaper's office in a well-preserved, long black car about twenty years old, with darkened windows, all of which should have been a clue to the adventure on which I was embarking. After thirty minutes of silence, I arrived at The Wilderness, a place properly named in all aspects, on a hot day with clouds moving in from the Gulf and air weighted heavily with moisture.

After her outburst that first day, Miss Royals primped her hair for a second and looked straight at me over the black feathers. "I expected they would do better, but I suppose I'll have to take what they sent," she said, and took a deep breath. I suspected she was reaching deep inside to pull up another insult, but instead, her explicit instructions came loud and clear. "My car will pick you up at eleven thirty, and you'll always arrive at twelve. We'll lunch first," she instructed. At that point, relinquishing the assignment entered my mind again, but that would have been tantamount to "giving up," and already spinning in my head were my mother's words, "Get to it!" and a slap on my butt usually followed.

Miss Royals was a small woman, thin with elbows and shoulders showing against the fabric of her dress. I guessed she was in her eighties. Her strange eyes were set deep, and her lips painted with the brightest red lipstick I'd ever seen; thick, pasty makeup covered her face and neck, and small saddlebags of skin hung from each jaw. "Lunch is ready," she announced. Her words were firm and commanding as her appearance as we stepped toward the dining room table.

Lunch was served that first day and each visit thereafter in the elaborate room reminiscent of television shows I'd seen about the rich and famous entertaining in fabulous apartments on Fifth Avenue in New York. Crystal and silver sparkled in candlelight, and gold-rimmed plates were carried by a rotund older gentleman wearing a black suit and white gloves. His mumblings sounded to be French, and Miss Royals replied likewise.

The windows were covered with heavy, dark curtains drawn closed, and always, she wore the "color of the day," she would say. For the next few weeks, sometimes her dress was dark, sometimes bright in a pastel color, with boas of feathers or flowing shawls of exotic fabrics, but always, from around her slim neck, dangled the same long gold chain set with emeralds, pearls, and diamonds. With each comment, the movements of her body and hands seemed calculated, as a great actress would do on a Shakespearean stage, and a deft red smile stayed locked on her face. Queen-like, she sat at the head of the table and spoke slowly, and with white-gloved hands, fingered her sceptre, a cane with a carved ivory handle. Soft, straight hair dyed black was set in swirls high on her head and crowned with a sparkling tiara. My place was always to her right, where, after lunch, I recorded every word, listened, and made notes while she told stories. Every now and then, she would point a finger straight to my face and with the same words each time, she'd exclaim: "You can only guess how it was back then, boy." Sometimes her words came out in sudden laughter, her gestures wide with hands as expressive as a ballerina's, and at other times tears gathered in her eyes, and sometimes, long sentences spewed buckets of pent-up anger and hate, long sentences that usually ended in a gasp for breath. Many times, I felt her anger was pointed straight to me, jarring me to quickly straighten up in my chair, raise my chin, and lock my eyes on hers.

That was my shield, my guard, and though meager, it was the only defense I had. And then suddenly, the lady would sigh deeply, letting the air hum out as though exhausted, and her eyes would roll back for a second. That, I learned, was the signal our tryst was over for the day.

After listening through six visits, her dismissal came when her finger pointed to me: "You've taken everything out of me, young man," she said, "so don't come back until you can bring the story and read it to me...show me what you've learned. Do you understand?" I stood quickly to gather up my belongings, and relief must have shown on my face. Her knuckles tapped the table. "Don't look so happy," she dragged her words demandingly, then began adjusting the emerald-and-pearl necklace. Slowly, her eyes turned up to mine and she asked: "Has anyone ever called you 'darkie' or 'colored?'" A sudden slap on my face would have stunned me less.

"Colored, yes, when I was a kid," I said, "but it's been a long time."

"Well, young mister colored boy," she said, emphasizing the word "colored," "this could be the last story you'll ever write around here."

I'd never examined closely my own feelings during the sessions, and when her dismissal came, I was shaken by her last words and felt more so that the prison doors had swung open, I'd been set free, the air was clean, and I could breathe. I also knew the rest was up to me, and I was certain that Miss Royal's story would be the onset of my lifelong career—I'd entered her past, her fears, and her inhibitions, inhibitions that I, too, had known something about, but had always kept myself above and beyond them. Nevertheless, I knew I lived somewhere in her story, having had many challenges similar to hers for having been cast as a dark-skin person. Relentlessly, I kept Miss Royals from knowing who I really was, how I felt; it was my story, too.

Four weeks later, I waited under the overhang in a cold December rain and watched an unshaven, stooped old man in threadbare clothes waiting under the shelter for the rain to slack. He glanced at me from under a rain-soaked cap, smiled slightly, and nodded, an omen of something good to happen, an okay, I hoped for a special blessing. I wanted to talk to him, tell him where I was going and what I was doing…I needed someone to listen, someone to tell, that I was on my way to the climax of an adventure that had started months before. Then a new limousine, long and white, slowly moved to the sidewalk in front of the office. I recognized the chauffer as he rounded the car and then opened the back door. "Reckoning day," I said softly and stepped to the car, my heart already thumping inside me while I grasped a green folder. I plopped onto the seat and was engulfed by the aroma of new leather. As the car moved slowly from the curb, the tattered old man raised his hand and smiled again…the blessing I needed, I was sure.

The twenty-mile drive to The Wilderness seemed longer than usual. Cold, misty rain fell continuously, and the wipers moved in a distinct rhythm to clear the glass. I looked at the green folder on the seat beside me, knowing that her words, spread over forty-five sheets, were my words now, arranged the way I wanted and the way I thought they'd best tell her story. The ancient trees with gray moss hanging from limbs sped by, while again, I debated the idea of handing the pages to Miss Royals and saying, "I'm sorry." I smiled and glanced through the dark window, knowing I'd have to walk those long twenty miles, and I was sure her lawyers would have me shot at sunrise the next morning. Then the desolate marshlands of tall brown grass in black water cast its loneliness, and I felt a hollow in my stomach. The iron runners on the white bridge sounded as they always had as the car crossed onto the island, and by the time silence came again, I'd made up my mind that what I had written was well done, and I would tell her what an honor it had been to write and I'd thank her. I felt my mother's hand then, with a slap on my bottom.

In the dining room, I sat at my place at the table, quickly glancing around the room. Miss Royals said nothing, but I felt her eyes watching my every move. I nibbled the food on my plate, and still glancing about, I knew something had changed in the big room; an aroma of flowers flooded the air, and I quickly searched to find what else was different.

During the usual silent lunch, I realized the dark curtains over the windows were open, making the crystal chandelier sparkle, the silver shine brighter, the room flooded with natural light, and I was startled again as much as the first time we met, seeing that Miss Royals's face was without the usual makeup; her eyes were blue, they were bright and were peaceful, her smile was soft and sure.

"Would you please read our story, young man?" she finally spoke, and smiled.

I opened the envelope.

* * *

MY LIFE
A story told by Miss Jesse Royals

In a misty rain on a Saturday morning, I left St. Louis at dawn on a smoke-filled train loaded with two hundred excited soldiers just out of the army in 1945. I was headed to a small town a hundred miles west of New Orleans, an old town named New Iberia. Arriving in midmorning the next day, Grandfather's driver, an older man I didn't remember, met me at the depot to take me the last twenty miles to The Wilderness, the home from which I'd been banned when I was eleven, fifteen years before.

We came first to the flat, green land with fences and animals grazing, big trees in front of small houses standing side by side; houses I remembered as a child and wished I were there with the children playing under the trees. Then we came to the dark water, the silent and mysterious marshland with tall grass that waved in the salty breeze from the ocean, and a few miles later, we approached the narrow bridge onto the island. My throat tightened and my stomach churned as the car moved slowly across the bridge's noisy iron runners. I remembered the sounds, frightening, like iron doors slamming, closing one after the other, and locking me in again.

A short way beyond the bridge, the car turned onto the narrow road leading into a thicket of briars, pine trees, and oaks, where remained the coolness of a morning fog. Deep inside the woods, we approached the iron gate, set between pillars of stone, from where a high rock fence extended far into the forest on both sides. The gate opened slowly, and I remembered my thoughts as a child, that this was the entrance into our castle, where the king lived, my king, who I feared, a powerful man who had locked me away from the children under the trees, and the rest of the world.

Beyond the gate, the landscape was the same as I remembered; the tops of the oak trees leaned awkwardly to the north, as did the pines, their nature twisted by the incessant winds from the ocean. I gasped for a breath, fighting back tears. The day had been brilliant, but right then, near noon, the road beneath the canopy was as dark as though the sun was setting. *A fall day near the sea,* came to mind, and I remembered, *days with no promise, no joy, no happiness, only salty wind that burned my cheeks and cut my lips.*

I watched the greenness through the car's window while wondering, recalling that through the years when friends at school inquired about where I was from, jokingly I'd say, "From Camelot, a long ways away." I knew even closest friends would never believe about a jungle near the ocean, and being reared by an old man and a mulatto woman we called Miss Hattie.

As the car moved slowly along the road, the life I'd left in St. Louis was blurred by everything I was seeing, a green prison with heart-wrenching memories of a misshapen childhood.

I thought about the old man and what he might be like after fifteen years, and wondered why he'd asked me to come, and then cursed myself that I had done so without question. *Maybe he's dying,* I thought. The words in Miss Hattie's letter had indicated urgency. *But maybe "dying" is merely an unspoken wish.*

A mile past the gate, we burst into sunlight with the lake in front of us, and then the sharp curve going left. On the other side of the lake, the big white house was daunting in its stance on the lake of dark water and massive old trees twisted by time and wind from the sea. Smoke from a chimney bloomed upward then fell onto the lake, where it glided softly like thin blue waves.

"Slow, please," I told the driver. I wanted to take in the puzzling beauty of the garden along the road, and there they were—bronze statues of deer ready to bolt into the dark woods; sheep never lifting their heads from the grass, and the birds in flight tethered to the ground by ribbons of wire—all were still there as they were when I left, still watching and waiting. And a hundred yards through the clearing, the big Buddha still ruled from his high pedestal, surveying his green domain. My throat tightened. And the twelve marble angels with pouting lips and folded wings stood as they always had, opposite one another along both sides of the road, beyond the deer, the sheep, the birds, and the Buddha. Softly, I spoke the name I'd given each one... my playmates, *the only friends I'd known.* I was saddened as I watched through the window; all these cold creatures that never moved, never made a sound, had waited in quiet stillness, but ready to run, to fly, to be let loose, to find life . *I had been one of them, all of us captives of an old man, my grandfather, who lived in the swirling void of madness.* I wiped a tear from my cheek.

The driver, old and stoic, had not spoken on the entire ride and had never glanced from the road in front of us. The car moved slowly. *And why did mystery always surround the simplest of things back then, and questions were shots fired in the dark because answers never came, except strange commanding sounds that most often forbid conversation beyond "yes, sir," or "no, sir."* I took a deep breath, vowing not to cry.

When the car reached the wide steps at the mansion's veranda, my palms were damp, and I doubted the wisdom of having come. The front door opened and Miss Hattie stepped onto the porch. She was tall, elegant as I remembered, and she wore a long, white robe. Serene and beautiful, she moved graciously across the porch and down the steps.

"It's safe now, Miss Jesse," she said as I stepped from the car. The air seemed heavy, salty, and smelled of dampness and green. Miss Hattie hugged me as the car pulled away, and the feel of her arms was soothing, warm, and familiar. Her soft brown hair with streaks of light was pulled back from her brown face, a kind face, her eyes sparkled with wetness. "Welcome home, Miss Jesse," she said, smiling. "Mister Royals will be pleased. You're a beautiful young lady."

"Thank you, Miss Hattie, and how is he?" I asked. Her aroma was the same I remembered as a child, when she rocked me and sang old hymns about Jesus and crossing over Jordan. I cried back then, because I felt so small, so lost and lonely in the trees and the wind. She would brush my hair from my face, press me to her breast, and soothe me: "Now don't you cry, Miss Jesse. Don't cry, my baby. Everything's gonna be all right," she'd say.

"You'll find him fairly well," Miss Hattie said, slightly smiling as we walked up the steps to the wide porch. "He cries out sometimes, maybe with pain, maybe with bad memories, but he refuses to leave The Wilderness or let the doctor come here...very hard headed." As the front door opened, her smile quivered for a second then she placed her hand on my arm. "He's looking forward to seeing you. I'm so glad you came," she said. "Please be kind to him." After fifteen years, I had forgotten the elegance of Miss Hattie's face, and seeing her at that moment, reminded me how badly I'd missed the only person whose love I'd ever felt.

"I'll be careful," I told her. "But why the urgency, Miss Hattie? It's been such a long time since I've been here, and he's never before asked that I come."

"He has a great deal to say," she said. "It's gonna take time for him to spill it all out, so you'll have to be patient... don't be weary with him, please, child."

We moved with my suitcase in hand into the foyer. I glanced around the skyward ceilings and long stairway of dark, carved wood, and on the first landing, daylight flooded a tall window where a million pieces of colored glass glistened, portraying a knight in armor with his eyes and his sword pointing downward overpowering anyone in front of him. Like the Buddha, the knight, too, had always struck fear inside me.

"Your room is waiting, Miss Jesse, and dinner will be served in a little while," Miss Hattie said.

The Wilderness. Then softly, I said the words, "The Wilderness," and I understood why the name felt right.

It was easy to see that the orderliness and formality of relationships had lingered in the house, and as I climbed the stairs, the fear I felt when a child in that dark place bubbled in my mind. *Hell, I'm twenty-five, and this is 1945. The whole world has changed, and I'm no longer part of this God-forsaken place!*

I sat on the edge of the bed and glanced around the room then lay back on the cover. All white, as it was the day I left, ceiling and walls, the bed covered with a white spread. *I was always lonely in here,* and I remembered feeling as though I was inside a cloud, afraid to move, afraid I'd stumble and fall into vast openness, into a deep, dark place, and at the bottom were pools of black water and twisted trees, wild wind that murmured endlessly in strange sounds, in voices I didn't know and in words I couldn't make out.

I glanced to the other side of the room to my desk holding books I'd studied till he sent me away. I remembered that day, the day we left. It was warm and at the end of spring when we boarded a train and he took me to a town in the middle of Missouri, a place I'd never heard of. And he left me there. I was eleven, and I hated him because I'd felt his scorn so often, and he was leaving me in a strange place with people I didn't know "to be educated for the world outside," he told the headmistress. As I looked at the books on the desk, I wanted to fan the pages for secrets and pieces of my childhood that might be scribbled there, but already I felt I was an intruder into a strange place and time.

Restless anger began bubbling inside me; *I am not the same person, the child he left in Missouri. I have friends and a future away from here, away from the old man and his craziness.* I wiped away the tears, sighed, and closed my eyes.

"Miss Jesse!" she said, and I jumped, startled from half-sleep. Miss Hattie stood in the bedroom door. "Dinner is ready. Be kind, child...he loves you." Those words, though gentle and sweet, I felt, were spoken as a warning.

He sat in his place at the head of the table. The old man wore a dark jacket over a white shirt and black tie, his white hair long and wiry, tall on his head, an appearance of anger and madness. He watched while I moved to the other side of the room. I passed the fireplace where a yellow flame struggled to burn and then sat to his right while his finger rhythmically tapped the table. Candles burned in silver holders. "Hello, Miss Jesse," he mumbled softly as I arranged myself in the chair. His eyes were stripping the skin from my face. "Welcome home."

"Thank you, Grandfather," I mumbled. "Good to see you." His eyebrows rose as though he had caught me lying.

Miss Hattie came with two gold-rimmed plates on a silver tray, set a plate in front of each of us then left the room with the same quick steps I remembered her always doing.

He coughed quietly. "This is Sunday, and Miss Hattie has taken the time to make you welcome," Grandfather said, speaking slowly and distinctly. "She's polished the silver and lit the candles, all for your coming, eager to make you happy, Miss Jesse. She's kind, a gentle person."

"Yes, sir," I stammered, refusing to smile. I wasn't hungry. After a few seconds, he broke the silence.

"Jesse, you're a grown woman now, and beautiful as I expected you would be. I hope your life is decent," he said.

"It is, Grandfather, I have friends from school and many at the bank where I work," I told him.

"Well," he said, and after a second, "a person can be labored by so-called friends and young men who present themselves as suitors. How about suitors, Miss Jesse? I know there's several lurking in the shadows."

"Yes, sir," I said quickly, "there *is* a young man, a lawyer."

"Is he a regular? Are you planning 'wedded bliss?'" he asked, his voice tipping up with sarcasm while his head moved jauntily.

"Yes, sir, we've talked about marriage, and I spent five days with his family during Hanukkah last December."

"Oh," he said, his eyes brightened. "A Jew? Damn!"

Damn is right, I thought. *I should have said 'no' to his question.*

"Well, my dear child, boyfriends and husbands can be dangerous; can create problems you don't need, not in *your* life. They can bring bad things out of a person, especially things that are nobody's business." He sat up straight, then leaned toward me, frowned, and pointed his finger. "Dangerous, Jesse. Dangerous." He glared for a second. "Get him out of your life, girl," he said, his eyes squinting. "You don't need him or anybody else, I can assure you."

"Yes, sir," I said. I wished I'd lied then; it was none of his business, and I hated his words. Anger and bitterness seeped up. I wanted to hit him.

"Jesse, I figure it's time we have an understanding about certain things; happenings making facts what they are in a frightening, cruel world." He looked away then, clearing his throat with a soft cough.

"Yes, sir," I said. I sighed deeply, waiting for his next move, which came only after several awkward seconds.

"I'm old now, Jesse," he said, his voice wavering as he looked at the fire. "Eighty-six in two weeks, if the good Lord okays it, and I feel death overtaking me." He spoke slowly. "I don't fear death, Jesse, but I have fear of life as it's going to be one day, fear about what's happening, changing the way we've always been. I sent you away to see the world outside, but now that the war is over, I'm fearful of so much change, and now, well, I figure you've seen enough that you should make your own judgement about what to do."

"Yes, sir," I said. I was lost in his rambling, and I hated the feeling that he had kicked me back to being *a child*. I shivered for a second in the quietness, in the dampness, in his presence. We continued our dinner, and my mind settled into the darkness as I recalled other nights, dinners when no words were spoken except reprimands to "sit up straight," "don't play with your food." My childhood fears were settling on me, and I remembered my only joy then was following the footsteps of Miss Hattie as she cleaned the house and cooked. After a few minutes, Miss Hattie returned and I wanted her to look my way so I could read her face.

"We'll move to the parlor in a few minutes, and I'll serve dessert there," she said, while busily clearing the table. I wanted her to somehow assure me with her eyes, but she never looked up, only glanced back and forth from her task to my grandfather. On her next trip back to the dining room, she helped the old man rise from his chair, took his arm and held it as he led the way to the parlor. There, a small fire burned, killing the damp chill in the room. He sat in a big chair facing the fireplace and motioned that I sit in the other. "I'll bring dessert," Miss Hattie said, and nodded as would a servant for her master's approval then left the room.

I could think of nothing to say to break the dreadful silence. I fidgeted with my hands; rampant thoughts with loose ends dangled in my mind. I wanted to run, get out of there, be sent to my room with a reprimand, anything would be better than closed in a room with the old man.

"Well," he said, his voice burst out, then he gasped for a breath of air. His words came out softly. "I understand you've made a place for yourself in St. Louis, doing very well at Mercantile Bank, huh?" He coughed. "You can work there forever if you like, I can assure you."

"Yes, sir, but menial work right now. Anybody can do it," I said. I felt as though I was willingly submitting to a beating. "Since the end of the war, there're a lot of men in the banking business, and it's impossible for a woman to get ahead."

"But you're tough, girl," he said. "You're a woman in a man's world, but I know your stock." His hand grasped tightly to the chair's arm while he coughed several times. I wondered how he knew so much about my work, about me, and what else he might know. His sermon continued for a couple minutes then quiet set in again. A dark, heavy blanket slowly began covering me, smothering me. I took a deep breath. The old man coughed just as Miss Hattie walked in.

"I'll come back in a little while to help you to bed, Mister Royals," she said.

"Thank you, Miss Hattie," he said softly. His eyes followed her to the door.

"She still lives in the log house out back?" I asked, my voice falling away.

"That's her home, Jesse," he said quickly and mean-like, then cut his eyes to me. "That's always been *her* home." Hate was in his words. His spectacles made his thin face appear small while magnifying deep wrinkles and puffiness. "And besides," he said, firmly, "that's where I started back there... that was my home...I set the first log in this dirt over fifty years ago." His breathing quickened and he frowned, his eyes still on me. "But I didn't bring you here to talk about Miss Hattie's house." He wrung his hands and winced as though in pain.

The old man showed no change in his lack of patience and quickness to anger. I was becoming upset with myself for being a submissive child again, and annoyed at him for being so strong and dominating. "Why am I here, Grandfather?" I asked quickly, my voice shaky. "I came because you asked me to come, but I still haven't figured it out." I wanted to speak out with something ugly and vile, anything to wake him up, make him talk openly and sanely.

"Calm down, girl," he said in a whisper, while squinting through his glasses. "I'm gonna tell you everything, keep you safe, but you gotta work with me, Jesse. Be kind now, girl, and try to understand. Believe me; it's important now, more than ever."

I glared at him. "Well, tell me why I'm here, why you sent for me, and don't say it was for reasons that aren't true. I want the real reasons." He glanced to the dwindling fire, took a deep breath, and shook his head.

"There's so much you don't know, Jesse, and it's time you learn about all of it. The good Lord made it this way for whatever reason he had," he said. "I have to make sure you understand it and you're willing to do what's necessary to keep things like they've always been. Do you hear me, Jesse? Understand me?" He sucked in a big breath, and then pointed a crooked finger at me. "People are mean, some might even kill you, and there's no way of changing from the way God did things."

I shivered at his words, hating him and regretting I'd made this useless trip.

He sat up straight in his chair then locked his hands together in his lap, then his thumbs twirled slowly around one another. He sighed deeply and coughed out the air.

I waited.

"When I was nineteen," he said while wiping the corners of his mouth with his napkin, and then shifting his eyes directly to me. I leaned toward him. "A young man by the name of Charles Duvalier married Kathleen Benoit not far from right here, 'bout twenty miles up the road. That was in the spring of 1879, and times were bad, everybody dirt poor, and the Carpetbaggers still here, hanging around and running everything."

He took out his handkerchief and wiped his brow, then refolded the handkerchief and returned it to his pocket. "I wanted to tell that boy how I felt about his marrying Kathleen...just a few words was all. Everything's not always what it seems, I'm afraid, and I knew Charles had been a mean boy who beat his hounds for no reason except they were dogs and killed animals for nothing except the excitement of feeling the power of a gun in his hand, and I expected he wouldn't change much after he married Kathleen. And too, with another mouth to feed and no work 'cept land work as it was back then, I suspected Charles Duvalier would get meaner than he was before." He pointed to the fireplace. "The fire," he mumbled, and motioned with his eyes. I got up and placed another log over the coals.

"After a rainstorm one day, I rode my horse out to where Charles and Kathleen lived, on a little place his daddy gave them as a wedding present. When I got to the cabin, I tied my horse at the steps and Kathleen came out onto the porch. She came down the steps and hugged me, then Charles stepped from the house, waving a pistol.

He cursed me and came to us, pointing the gun straight at me. I grabbed for the pistol just when Kathleen stepped between us. It fired and Kathleen fell to the ground. Charles looked at the pistol in his hand, then at Kathleen trembling on the grass. He screamed like a panther and threw the gun down then ran into the woods. I put Kathleen in a wagon and took her to her momma and daddy's house. The next day, Kathleen and the baby inside her died." With the handkerchief from his pocket, the old man wiped his eyes then started again.

"Three days later a posse went out to look for Charles in the tangles of briars in the deep woods and swamp. I was one of the men in that group, and I was the one who found him hiding up in a tree, and I shot him right there, before the others caught up with me." Hearing his words, I winced and wondered what other secrets he might reveal.

The parlor door opened. "Well, y'all have talked enough for now," Miss Hattie said as she eased her way to stand between Grandfather's chair and mine. "Miss Jesse, you know the way to your room, child. I hope you sleep well after that long trip." Grandfather sighed. "Oh, enough for now, Mister Royals," Miss Hattie told him. "You all can talk some more in the morning."

The dark and quietness in The Wilderness ate at me. The old house was musty. The bark of a dog far off was unsettling, as was the scream of a small animal caught in the jaws of a predator. All the scents and sounds settled inside me, dark and wet, and for a second, I shivered. Through the windows, I could see the tall trees as they danced in the moonlight. I needed to sleep; I wanted to cry and there was no one I could touch. Finally sleep came, dark, troubled sleep, making me fearful and restless in twisted dreams.

"Good morning, Miss Jesse," Miss Hattie said. She smiled as she placed a cup and saucer on the side table. "It's nine o'clock and your grandfather'll be waiting for you on the front porch in a little while. I'll bring your breakfast there." She left my room.

On the porch, I sat in the rocker next to the old man. "Good morning," I said. He gazed in front toward the lake, his eyes glassy, appearing to see nothing. He cleared his throat.

"In 1896," he said, surprising me, beginning so quickly, "this land was given to me by the government, the document signed by Mister Theodore Roosevelt," he said. "Forty acres was all, and now I own this whole island, the salt mines and the oil wells...every bit of it."

"Good morning, again, Miss Jesse," Miss Hattie said. "I hope you slept well last night."

"I did," I said, lying. She set the tray on my lap, turned, and re-entered the house.

"And after I killed Charles Duvalier, the sheriff locked me up," Grandfather said, still with glassy eyes fixed over the lake. "I explained that it was him or me that day in the woods, and I was the one with a gun, and I made sure Charles Duvalier would never tell the story. They let me go." A tear ran down a fold in his cheek. "I lived in the woods on government land for three years till Mister Roosevelt gave me these forty acres where we sit right now." He cut his eyes to me then, as though expecting a response. I looked at the old man but said nothing. I nibbled my food.

He looked down, then brushed his lips with his fingers. "After Mr. Roosevelt deeded me this land, I figured me and the rest of the world, too, would be best-off if I stayed right here in The Wilderness."

"Was Kathleen carrying your baby, Grandfather?" I asked snidely, hoping to catch him off guard. He raised his chin and again, cast his eyes to the lake. His breathing quickened. "Was that your baby, Grandfather?"

"Yes!" he yelled. "That was my child, and Kathleen was gonna marry *me*." He slammed his hand onto his chest. "Me," he said softly. Then he closed his eyes as he laid his head on the back of his chair.

"Why didn't you marry?" I asked and watched his face redden more.

"Her daddy believed I was a gypsy, and he forbade her to see me," he spoke softly, then stopped as if waiting for me to ask something. He blinked several times to clear his eyes and began again. "When I was about four years old, my daddy died in the war when the Union Army took over Vicksburg where we lived. When I turned eleven, my momma and both my sisters died from the fever. A gypsy family took me in, and they gave me a new name: Harman Royals. I went wherever they went; sometimes we'd spend the winter in Texas. We'd spend summers roaming in the North, but it didn't matter where we went, people never liked us to be there. The gypsies were dark skinned. One winter we came to these parts, down here in this wilderness. I was sixteen then, and I was tired of all the moving and everybody always threatening and mean toward us."

The old man raised his head and looked straight in my eyes. "This is the kind of country here where people like their kind, too, Jesse, just like everywhere else I went with the gypsies. We weren't welcome here either. We were looked down on, considered nothing more than dust, never trusted, and forbidden to leave the woods even to buy food. We had a hard time that winter. When the family left to go north in the spring, I stayed behind. I lived in a barn on Kathleen's daddy's place and worked for him, and that's how I come to know her. The gypsies never came back."

"Oh, Grandfather, I'm sorry," I said. I wondered about truth in his story.

"The gypsies are just about the only family I remember, Jesse, and I learned a lot while I lived with those folks, about how people look at you and treat you if you look different from them." He squirmed in his chair then brushed a speck from his pant leg.

"Grandfather," I said quickly, "this is the first I've known about your life, and I know nothing about my mother and father—nothing...not even the slightest bit about who they were. Why haven't you—?"

"No, Jesse," he shot back, his brows fixed, his eyes straight to my face. He sat upright in his chair. "Till now, you've been too young to understand or you lived away. I'm gonna get to it."

I wanted to scream at him, but I knew to do as Miss Hattie had said, "Don't get weary of him." He rocked in his chair and hummed for a few seconds, gathering his thoughts, then looked at me. His bleached-white skin and deep grooves across his cheeks and forehead frightened me.

"I got a poor sort of memory now," he mumbled. "I gotta find bits and pieces of things and put them together. You have to be patient with me, girl."

"That's okay, Grandfather. I'm sorry," I said. Truly, I was sorry he recognized my impatience and discontent.

"A few years after Kathleen died, I got this land. This was the first of everything I own, and I vowed I'd take care of it and it would never be taken away. It was protected by the marsh on three sides and the sea on the south." Loudly, he cleared his throat. I figured Miss Hattie would make him go inside if she heard him.

"After crossing the Vermillion River one day, I came to an opening about fifteen miles up from here. My horse shied and wouldn't calm down, kept backing away, so I got off him to look a little ways up the road. Lying in the tall grass to the side was a young girl, barely alive, her clothes mostly torn off. She had scratches and cuts on her face and arms. The ants and bugs had already started eating on her fingers where the blood was. As best I could, I cleaned her up and fed her some crackers and gave her water from my canteen, but when she opened her eyes and saw me, she screamed and tried to fight me. I held her to me till she calmed. She was beautiful, Jesse, had light skin and her hair was soft. She was only fourteen she told me."

"When was that, Grandfather?" I asked. He seemed happy at that moment, content. But I struggled with anxiety. I was sure I recognized the young girl he'd described.

"By then, Jesse, I owned this island, and the salt mines were operating...around 1918." His voice was gravelly. Miss Hattie handed each of us a glass of tea. She looked at Grandfather, watching every movement. He sipped from his glass, then smacked his lips. She smiled when he looked up at her.

"You're doing fine, Mister Royals," she said, nodding and smiling, "just fine."

"Certainly, Miss Hattie, thank you." He glanced up again, then shook his head. "I'm gonna finish this story, Miss Hattie, while I got the pieces together." She left us on the porch.

"I brought that girl here to my place, to The Wilderness. I told her she could live here and be safe. She could take care of this house and help me. Sometime later, Jesse, she told me she was mulatto, and that's why some men beat her and left her to die on the side of the road."

"Why?" I asked, frowning. "And beat her? Why would they do such a thing?"

"She was too white to be colored, and in these parts down here, she was too dark to live as a white person," he said. He hesitated for a second, glanced at me, and continued: "But she drew comfort from all I did for her, and I took comfort too, because I done good by Miss Hattie, and she stayed with me all these years."

My mind was firing one thought after the other as the old man spoke and became eager to ask questions. I moved out of the bright sun into the shade. He sipped his tea then set the glass on the table beside him. "How about my parents, Grandfather?" I asked quickly.

"No, no, no, Jesse!" he said, shaking his head and frowning. I wondered if he'd continue. I was determined to make him tell me about my mother and father. I fired another question.

"Let's talk about my dad, your namesake," I said quickly. "Why don't you tell me about him?" He closed his eyes and raised his face straight to the brightness of the morning sun. A tear slid down a crease in his cheek. "And my mother, Grandfather, what was she like?" He looked straight at me then.

The screen door to the porch opened and Miss Hattie walked toward us. "Time to eat dinner, you two," she said, standing almost at attention at Grandfather's side, her hands clasped together. Grandfather looked at Miss Hattie and raised his hand. She took it in hers.

"Not now, Jesse. Not now," he said softly, barely audible. "We have to eat for Miss Hattie right now." His breaths were short. He looked up to Miss Hattie's face. She smiled and smoothed his hand with hers, their eyes met. At that instant, the air became heavy and my breathing stopped as I recalled how dreadfully Miss Hattie wept the day he told me my parents had been killed in a race riot in New Orleans. She had held me to her so tightly I could barely breathe. Then I cried, too, for her.

After lunch and a rest for Grandfather, we returned to the porch and watched a dozen white geese play at the edge of the lake beyond the road at the porch steps. He'd smile at times, pensive mostly, and appearing that his mind was gathering more pieces as it wandered through his years. Looking closely at the wrinkled white skin, the gnarled fingers, and hearing the heartache in his stories, I realized the old man had never overcome the terrors of his own childhood during the Civil War, alone in his youth and the times of a long life, and now, he was turning them loose. As I scolded myself for being annoyed and sometimes impertinent, I was suddenly struck with the feeling that my mind was yielding to a subtle persuasion being put upon me by the old man.

He wrung his hands together for a few seconds, folded them in his lap, and never took his gaze from the geese on the lake.

He cleared his throat then started speaking, slowly and soundly. "A few weeks after you were born, Miss Jesse, I was sitting right here listening to the evening sounds, when six lights appeared in the darkness on the other side of the lake at the curve. I watched two of them coming to the house and knew what was happening. I called to Miss Hattie to bring my gun, and when she came out of the house, she knew also what was getting ready to take place. I told her to go back inside and lock the door, but she refused to move from my side. In no time, two riders in white robes and hoods stopped their horses right here at these steps." The old man stopped, raised his arms as though aiming a gun. "I was ready," he said, "to kill both of them, right there," and he pointed to the ground at the bottom of the steps. "Then one started talking, a voice I knew right off," he said, and then brought his arms down. "He told me they knew I was hiding two half-breeds here in The Wilderness, and said he was giving fair warning that they should be kept out of sight, outside the community, and away from town. And he told me they'd be back on another day. That's when I should have pulled the trigger, but Miss Hattie's hand took my arm, and she whispered, 'Don't do it. We'll take care of it.'"

My mind whirled, and I gasped. He spoke quickly.

"Jesse," he said softly, as he turned to look straight at me. I watched his eyes and lips. I heard, "Jesse" again, and I knew right then and there, his next words would devour me. "You can return to St. Louis if you wish and live there as a white woman with no history." His eyes moved back to the geese. "Or, you can stay here in The Wilderness and live your life as a rich woman, as a puzzle with a few missing pieces, but safe from a mean world."

My breaths were short but coming fast. "What the hell are you saying?" I screamed, knowing then that everything the old man was—his hate, his prejudices, and his fears—were laid out in front of me, and like chains, they had bound me to him—and to this place—The Wilderness.

He turned facing me, and tears came to his eyes, but I felt no sorrow for him.

My breathing quickened, and I wanted to kill him. I stood quickly, my fist ready to pound his face when Miss Hattie's arms surrounded me. Tears were in her eyes, and looking into her brown face was like seeing my own in a timeless mirror. She pressed me to her, consoling me, as a mother would do upon finding her lost child. She wept. "Yes," she whispered. "Yes."

A week before Christmas, my mother wrapped my father in a blanket and held his hand while they watched the white geese on the lake. He fell asleep, and we couldn't wake him.

* * *

I adjusted my blue jacket and the striped tie I'd bought for the occasion of reading what I'd written. Then I cut my eyes to Miss Royals and took a deep breath, wondering how I should react if she hated the story.

During the entire time I read, I was aware of the lady's constant examination, her eyes moving from my face to my hands and back again. Often I'd glance and she'd be smiling and other times she'd wipe away a tear. It was impossible for me to figure what thoughts ran rampant through her mind.

I closed the pages and handed them to her. She held them loosely, her hand on the table, glancing at the sheets then back to me, as though wondering if they were worth keeping. I expected her to say anything, possibly something ugly and mean, and I was prepared to hear the worst with my mind spinning like a top. Hoping to quell the anxiety, I took in the changes in the big room one more time.

She cleared her throat, and my eyes settled on her face. Her lips moved, forming words that didn't come out, then tears came. After a couple seconds, she smiled. Her voice was soft, clear, and the words came out slowly.

"Your story ends when I came back to The Wilderness in 1945," she said, meekly.

"Yes, ma'am, but you didn't give me anything about yourself after that time," I said, somewhat apologetically. I waited for her to suddenly become enraged.

"No," she whispered. "So much ended then, and there was nothing to tell." She scanned the colorful rug in front of us for a second then looked back to me as she pressed her hand onto her forehead. Her eyes were blue, clearly blue, a final determination I made at that moment, and she focused them on my face. "Acceptance of the wrongs others have done to you is difficult, but forgiveness is not impossible, and that may take a lifetime." She glanced down for a second then raised her chin. "Sadly, all I've done in my life is breathe." Then she touched her cheek where a tear had run. Her words made sense to me, and I felt her pain, and better understood the anger she had exhibited on earlier visits. For the first time in the weeks I'd known her, her face was peaceful. Her eyes brimmed with tears and newness, obviously with secrets, and certainly questions. The first one hit me: "And what's it like out there, young man, for a person with brown skin?"

She blindsided me, I thought, hating I'd let down my guard. I hesitated to say anything. I grimaced and took a deep breath, nervously fearful because that was a question I'd never been asked so bluntly.

"What's it like out there for a young man like you, a young man whose name I've never heard?" she asked, a slight smile on her face, her finger softly touching her lips.

"I'm an American, ma'am, third generation," I said. "And times have changed, and people have changed."

She shook her head, smiling as her chin rose then her eyes again looked squarely into mind. She spoke slowly. "I was afraid of change because my father insisted I should be. Now I see that every generation knows fear when they recognize 'change' around them. But in the scheme of time, our memories are very short...our life on earth is short... permitting the evolution of mankind and culture to proceed slowly so we don't destroy each other and our world." She raised her hand slightly and pointed her finger at me.

"A thousand times in dreams, I've walked along a street and saw myself in a life I could have lived, and then, when the dream was over and daylight came, I was still who I am, and now, an old woman hiding in The Wilderness, waiting...like 'the deer, the sheep, and twelve silent angels' you've described so aptly in our story."

I couldn't help but feel pity then for the lady and felt I should say something kind, a feeling that until then was rare, and I had no words to express it.

"You *are* who you are," she continued. "It's obvious." She smiled. "But time and people can warp you even when you like yourself." Her hands shook slightly, and she smiled. "I've never had friends to come my way, but you have opened my life as you've passed through my secret world." She brushed her fingers over her brow, her head tilted. "My father lived a long life and was never able to justify what changes were taking place, and in his mind, I was a living testament to all his prejudices and fears, believing that no one would ever approve of his love for me or my mother, a black woman. Poor fellow." She looked past me for a second. As it happened, I glanced to my hands, then back to Miss Royals. She was smiling.

She raised her opened hand and held it beside her caramel face. "You see," she said, glancing back and forth from her hand to me, "browning started long ago, young man, long before *I* came along and certainly long before you were born." She hesitated, a slight smile on her face. "And I think 'amalgamation' may be a fine word in today's lexicon, don't you think...to help explain that *the browning* is natural, nature's way of ever so slowly moving us into the future, maybe taking several hundred years, possibly a thousand?"

I wanted to say something, anything. "Maybe you're right," I said. "But I've just never thought about it very much."

She continued, "I suppose historians will someday write that the browning was a great catalyst to peace in the world." Then, her long fingers fluttered beside her face, her smile was slight. "Look at this, young man...we're ahead of time. We're a 'preview,' you and me...the color our country and the whole world will be some day," she said as the tenor of her voice rose. Her smile was genuine, and she chuckled then quietly sighed as though exhausted.

My heart beat fast as I skipped down the front steps to the car. I had survived; that was the important thing, and my confidence was exploding. As the car eased around the lake, I fingered her approval letter, laughed out loud, and then it hit me: I'd never told her my name...and as the limousine glided along the smooth asphalt, I was shaken by the startling change in the garden landscape...the bronze deer had bolted into the forest, the grazing sheep had wandered into greener pastures...

And I never told her my name? "My name is Edward," I yelled to the driver.

The tethered birds had been set free...

"Please tell her for me—it's Eduardo—my name is Eduardo O'Reilly."

...and the twelve silent angels had returned to God.

THE LAST DAFFODIL

My hero? You want me to tell about my hero? ...Oh, darlin', it'd be my pleasure...I'd love to because my brotha was my hero, and has been for all my life. Bless his heart...he'd rise from the dead if he could hear us talkin' 'bout him...he never wanted to be the center of attention, not him, not Adam. That was his name, Adam...and I guess it's okay for my brotha to be my hero, don't you think so, darlin'? ...Oh, wonderful!

Well...a long time ago...oh, I'll just talk about him, sweetheart, if that's all right...Okay...Poor boy...Adam stayed angry till the day he died, because early on everybody teased him about his hangin' on Momma's breast till he was right at six years old...a big ole boy doin' that. Sometimes he'd hide...but it made him a momma's boy, I'm pretty sure. Honey, he never grew past the meanness of all that teasin'... he was still a boy in a lotta ways when he passed nearly sixty yeahs ago; only sixteen, that's all, so awful young, and so innocent. You know, he neva saw past these cotton fields around heah, neva saw a mountain, or the ocean...he never saw the ocean...oh, my...and that makes me wanna cry. Everybody ought to see the ocean when they're little and it's so big, but Adam died too soon, poor boy...never kissed a pretty girl either, that I know of...and I'd bet my life on it, that it was the girls who missed out. And I don't mean to sound melancholy, darlin'...but to me it's sad that he neva had a girl to wrap his arms 'round to make love to...poor Adam...it just distresses me to think about how much he missed out on. And he was such a good boy, too, and I love him still, but you know somethin'...it's been so long ago, all I can see of him now are his eyes...those blue eyes in the sun looked like crystal marbles...the kind of marble that'd be just right for your taw, and you could see all the way through those eyes, straight to his soul...it's sad now. And you do know what a "taw" is, don't you? Good. And his voice...well, I don't hear it anymore, darlin'. It's gone from me, and I hate that. Oh, that's a shame, don't you think so... when you start forgettin'...forgettin' your own people, the ones you loved...nearly a sin I guess you could say, but that's the way it is, I guess...anyway....

Long before he passed, Adam was already my hero. Let me tell you, though...Daddy said he was "bedeviled." Daddy used to tell Momma that all the time, since the day poor Adam got his arm broke, broke right below the elbow, when he was about ten. Momma told me all about it...our Daddy did it, the rascal...and Daddy didn't want to take him to the doctor because he couldn't pay him...that's what Daddy said anyway, and said Adam was bedeviled. But later on, me and Momma figured Daddy said Adam was bedeviled for a lot of reasons...because Adam came durin' that awful time, that terrible depression when everybody was so poor, didn't have a thing...at least my family didn't, anyway. Daddy said hard times was killin' him long 'bout then, and there came Adam...and poor Momma...she said she nearly died. Daddy said it was an omen for somethin', Momma being so sick and

The Last Daffodil

all, and Adam being so beautiful at the same time. Momma said people came from miles around to see her beautiful baby and everybody just loved him...daffodils were bloomin' 'bout then, everywhere, and they all brought daffodils to Adam, like the whole world was celebratin'. After two or three days, the house was filled with flowers, with sweetness and "even the air was yellow," Momma said. But Daddy said it was a God-awful time for Adam to come into the world when it seemed like the whole world was dyin' all around 'um. So...maybe Adam *was* bedeviled. I don't know about that, but to me Adam was fine, handsome, and still beautiful when he died...and so said the girls at school, too...and I don't mind tellin' about him, because he's still my hero to this very day.

And the way God took 'im; oh, my...a sad story, but I don't blame God, mind you; just sad, that's all. Well, it was cool that mornin' in March, but by the time we left for the lake, the sun was comin' on pretty strong. Even so...ridin' in the back of Daddy's old truck was chilly, and the wind was whippin'. Adam didn't say anything, and I didn't either, but I could tell he was happy 'bout his birthday and goin' to the lake. I just admired him; he was *so* handsome, what I call, a "pretty boy"...and I believed he didn't like me watchin' him...not under normal circumstances mind you...but with the wind blowin' and everything, I don't reckon he noticed me lookin' at him right then. His hair was flyin' and he just let it go *wild*, and needless to say, Daddy hated Adam's long hair, blond and curly. You can imagine. And that was the least of things Daddy fussed at Adam about; but Adam never showed out any, just stayed silent when

Daddy carried on about him. At regular times, Adam was a quiet young man, kept to himself. In fact, Daddy said he was "closed-up," and Momma said he was betrayin' everybody by lockin' everybody out, but worse than that, she said he was betrayin' himself...*losin' his soul* by not drawin' to God. Poor Momma...she figured her words were holy if she put God somewhere in what she said, but I was just ten and didn't know anything, really, and Adam never caused *me* any trouble or locked *me* out; and about God and all...well, like I said, I was just ten, darlin'.

It was Adam's sixteenth birthday that day, and I hadn't told him I had him a present, a poem I'd written, and a little story about my cat. He liked poems and stories—those blue eyes would light up, and he'd smile the whole time he read. Really, Adam was *more* than just *any* boy, and I remember that. And he was six years older than me, and his full name was James Adam Bowie, almost like the real James Bowie. Oh, my...he never liked to be called that, though, because it...well, he thought James Bowie was a hero, why he died at the Alamo and all, and Adam never figured *he* was anybody's hero. He took "Adam" as his name, but Momma and Daddy called him by the name they give to him...James Adam. And Momma and Daddy were the ones closed-up, the way I saw it, not Adam. I guess that's not nice to say about the people who gave you life, but anyway...if anybody'd ever ask me if somethin' was wrong with my Momma and Daddy, I'd say, "yes...just about everything." That's the way I felt... most of the time, anyway.

Well...on the way to the lake that day, Daddy turned off the main road onto a little dirt road that was on a ridge goin'

The Last Daffodil

to higher ground, a natural rise...straight into a thicket of pine trees that were so tall you couldn't make out the tops of 'um. He'd already told Momma we were goin' on one of his expeditions before we got to the lake, but not to tell Adam because then he wouldn't wanna go...and he'd cause trouble. That's what Momma told me. That's what she said.

Well, when the truck left the road, I saw Adam's lips move, sayin' plainly a bad word, and he shook his head and looked at me, then he said somethin' else not loud enough for me to hear. Nobody liked Daddy's expeditions, not even Momma, but there was no doubt who led the charge when Daddy rode the horse...you know what I mean, darlin'?

Adam said Daddy knew every old shack in the woods for miles around, and who lived in 'um one time, whose wife somebody stole from 'um, and who made the "shine." That day, though, Adam sat in the back of the truck across from me, sort of talkin' to himself, like I said, and he just spoke that one bad thing when Daddy left the road. I was glad about that, 'cause ugly words always upset me, I guess because Daddy used so many when he was overtaken.

Adam and Daddy were really separated...wide apart, you know what I mean? And I figured that was a bad thing. Momma said Adam might outgrow it one day when he got older or found him a girl. I didn't know, I really didn't, not about that, and Adam was such a gentle young man, so sweet, and I don't say that just because he was my brotha, but because he was. He was just kind and sweet...just that way.

Well, it was beautiful and nice under those tall pines where Daddy stopped the truck...the air smelled so clean, fresh, and untainted, and I heard music, God's music...like in church. And some other trees had thick, shiny leaves and pale little flowers hanging over 'um. Anyway, I stood up and looked around. I wanted to cry there, it was so wonderful... the way the mornin' sun broke through the trees, lit up the ground in long streaks, and I was sure, then, that that was a place God had waitin' for somebody, and somethin' really special; all around on the ground there were yellow flowers bloomin' up through the pine straw. Daffodils, I remember, just everywhere...decorated with daffodils...oh, darlin', only God himself could have done it that way.

Anyway, when the truck stopped, Adam jumped over the side and stood there, and all of a sudden, some crows started callin'; really made me feel bad that they'd be in God's beautiful temple. And they were mockin' God, I could tell, screamin' and fussin' because God had brought my family to his temple that mornin'. That's what went through *my* mind. I never liked crows...so black...like death...maybe an omen for somethin' bad. But anyway...

Then Daddy stepped out the truck, struck a match, and I smelled the cigarette all the way to where I was. "I use to ride over here regularly when I was young," Daddy said, and he looked straight at Adam, and Adam's eyes rolled back. "To an old graveyard," Daddy said, his eyes glassy, left over from the night before.

Adam shook his head. I thought for a minute Daddy might remark something at him, but he didn't, and I was glad. Poor Adam...all he wanted, really, was for Daddy to love him, at least a little, and all Daddy wanted was for Adam to love him back. Well, that's what I thought, but like I said, I was just ten.

The crows screamed again, and Daddy looked around like he was trying to find somethin' familiar to right the place in his mind. Adam whispered to me. "He's lying, Sister. This is where he made the 'shine,' him and his friends, where the law couldn't find him."

"No," I told him quick like, figuring if Daddy heard Adam say somethin' like that, no tellin' what he'd do, might kill Adam right there in that temple. And you know what? Adam was the first to admit he brought bad things on himself when it came to Daddy, and Daddy would call him ugly names...names that made Momma cry.

"Okay, let's look around," Daddy said like an order. He only *glanced* toward Adam that time. I suspected he was temptin' Adam to say somethin' ugly.

Daddy looked sad right then, standin' by the truck, real down 'bout somethin' or other...sad lookin', and it reminded me of the look Adam took on when Daddy hit him, and that's when he'd say that poem, always the same one...he'd just stand straight up recitin' those words over and over and gettin' louder every time Daddy cut that strap 'cross him. I use to say it with Adam. I still know it now... at least part of it, somethin' Adam wrote one day:

> *And who am I to stand so bold...*
> *Just a boy that God did mold,*
> *Yet a stranger crying and afraid,*
> *In a lonely world I never made.*

I still say those words, darlin', can you believe that? At real special times when I feel like I'm fallin' down, fallin' into an abyss where it's dark and wet. It's a prayer, I do believe, because Adam said so, a prayer about him, but he said Daddy never heard it and God must not have cared. Most often, Daddy cried, too, while he swung that strap with Adam sayin' those words and lookin' straight in Daddy's eyes.

Anyway, when Momma stepped out the truck in God's temple, she sighed and cut her eyes to Adam when she went by, and she fixed her hat tight on her head. I tapped Adam's arm.

"Come on," I told my brother, and before I knew what happened, he shoved me in the back, knockin' me to the pine straw way up in front. He just stood where he was, and his face twisted like somebody stabbed him with a sharp blade, or shot him, then his eyes blinked. He looked around that temple for a second, then closed his eyes till he looked to his feet, and my eyes followed his, and that's when I saw it, too, its tail going under the pine straw. I looked at Adam's face, white as a sheet, and before I could scream, Adam spoke softly. "I'm sorry, Sister," his lips said real plain, and he hushed me with his finger up to his lips. To this very day, it's hard for me to *think* about what Adam did that mornin' for me, and God never justified it either, not to me, anyway. I cry every time it comes to mind, you know what I mean? I still feel sorry for Adam.

After a few seconds, Adam helped me up from the ground, and went and sat on the tailgate of Daddy's truck, just sat there swingin' his legs. I asked him if he was gonna tell Daddy about it, and asked him if it hurt.

"No," he said, and he shook his head real slow. "You go with them, Sister." He never called me anything but "Sister."

"I'll stay with you, Adam," I told him and sat by him. I started cryin', and he patted my leg. He smiled a little and looked at me like he was glad I stayed, and that's when I gave him the poem I'd written for his birthday. He read it and smiled, then I asked him again if it hurt. He never answered and after a couple seconds, he closed his eyes.

When Daddy's voice rang through the trees, it frightened me, and I wanted to cry. "Get your butt over here, James Adam," he had yelled, and I believe the whole temple shook. Adam wiped his eyes with his fist then pressed his fingers to his lips; already, they were swellin'.

"You go, Sister," he said soft like. When I glanced back, Adam was curlin' up on the tailgate, placin' one hand under his cheek.

When I got to where Momma and Daddy were waitin', Momma said, "Look, Cotton, at all the yellow flowers." But right then I couldn't see color...there was no color at all, everything was gray and brown, the trees, the flowers, Momma's face...and the air was damp and hard to breathe.

"There are eight graves here, Cotton," Daddy said, looking straight at me, then he glanced toward Momma standin' by me with her hands locked together, her eyes wet... almost cryin'. I knew then that this place was no temple... God wasn't there, either, not that I could tell.

Well, anyway, "Cotton" is a name Daddy gave me because my hair turned white in summer, from the sun. I don't believe I told you that, did I? Adam use to say I was the white-haired angel holdin' up the "Eye of God" in the front of our family Bible, and he was the other angel, the one without wings. That's what he said, really, and I used to be afraid when I looked at that eye, it was so big, right in the middle of a triangle, and it would cut right through me it seemed like. Adam just laughed, though. We laughed sometimes, Adam and me, about a lotta things, about angels with no wings, and God. Anyway...

Almost in tears, Momma spoke real soft, "Oh, poor Mary," like she was a friend of the person under that deep layer of brown pine straw. Then I saw the headstone she was lookin' at: *Mary, age eight, 1917*. Momma glanced at every headstone. "All died at the same time," she said straight to me, like she really wanted me to know that, and then she sighed and nodded when Daddy pointed to another headstone. "Look at that, Cotton," she said softly.

"That's what I wanted James Adam to see, Cotton," Daddy said, then he asked where Adam was. Daddy wobbled a little then, and braced his self against a tree. "He's in the truck," I told him, but I couldn't look at Momma or Daddy, not in their gray faces, anyway. Instead, I looked at my brotha's *full name* carved in that headstone Daddy was standin' over. I knew Daddy was bad off by the way he talked and the way he held to that tree, and Momma and I watched him suck the last drop out the bottle, then he pitched it as far off as he could.

"Damn," he said and kept *shakin'* his head. "I brought him here to see this, for his birthday, so he'd know where he got his name, from a real man." Daddy was almost cryin', like he was a lot of times late at night, and I didn't know what to say, and Momma wiped her eyes.

"I gave him my Daddy's name, right there," Daddy said and pointed again. That's what he said, like it was a big thing, which I guess it was to him, and then he looked at me. "Cotton," he said, and shook his finger toward me, "these are your people, girl, my family, and God let the flu get all of 'um while I was soldiering 'cross the ocean, took everybody...every one of 'um." He started cryin' and sat on the ground by his daddy's grave. "I was sixteen when I left home and had no family when I got back, a home neither," he said. Then Momma sat down by him and placed his head in her lap. Momma used to say Daddy and Adam were just alike, they needed somebody to love and their nature was drownin' 'um because they never figured out themselves, or each other...poor souls.

Daddy tried to wake Adam that mornin' on the tailgate, but couldn't.

"I hope Adam's happy now," Momma said after I told 'um why he pushed me down, "and in heaven...even with his dyin' *on purpose.*" That's what she said.

Daddy said it was just like Adam, "...dyin' so to get the last word in."

I brought flowers to Adam that mornin' darlin'...daffodils.

And I hope God'll rest their souls if he can, 'cause they're all together now; Momma, Daddy, and Adam are side by side in that old graveyard, but darlin', I quit goin' there a long time ago because I heard whispers and voices, and crows callin', and I cried every time I went because all the daffodils were gone.

SPECIAL ARRANGEMENTS AT MICKEY SPITZER'S

My little old radio went static for a couple seconds, then a man came on and said a war was startin' way off somewhere on the other side of the Pacific Ocean. Then another man came on and said 1950 was gonna be the hottest summer we ever had in these parts. That's when I wiped my face with my sweat rag, and just when I put it around my neck, I saw him standin' where you turn to come up our path to the house. He sure didn't look anything like a dog I'd pick out if I had a chance. I was sittin' in the shade on the steps and he started walkin' real slow, like Momma says, "just pussyfootin' around," walkin' like he had no purpose a' tall. When he saw me, he stopped and looked for one little second, then his tail went straight up and started movin' from side to side. That's when he started runnin' to me like I was the one he'd been tryin' to find.

Well, I saw right off he was a skinny old dog and his hair was a funny color, yellow, and he had a black nose. When he got close enough for me to hear him whine the way he did, I figured he was tellin' me he was *sent*, and I said right off, "Thank you, God, for sendin' me a dog." Momma said that was the only way I'd ever get a dog, if the Lord himself sent one, and Momma said it had to be a boy dog, too, because there weren't no way we could raise a bunch of offspring. And when that yellow dog got to the steps, I stood up and he laid down right in front of me and whined, like he was awful ashamed, and tellin' me he was sorry for whatever it was he did, then he rolled on his back with his legs straight up. That's when I could tell he was a boy. He sure wasn't scared either, but with that yellow hair, I figured he oughta be. I told him I was scared sometimes, and my hair wudden yellow. I asked him if he was hungry and when I got up to go inside, he jumped up and followed me. "Stay right there," I said, and he sat outside the screen door. Right then, I didn't know what to call that funny-lookin' dog.

Now, my momma worked at the County Home for old white folks. They went there when they got sick or lost their minds. Momma said some just got so old they couldn't take care of their selves. She liked working there, and been there since before Daddy left. Well, I don't rightly know what happened 'bout my daddy, not yet anyway, but Momma said she'd tell me one day when I got old enough, about my daddy, and about me gettin' a dog. Heck, right then, I was gonna be nine before school started, and I been stayin' all by myself while Momma worked, so I figure I been old enough for at least two years now.

Anyway, I found some leftover biscuits on the stove, broke one up in a bowl, and poured a little bit of milk over it. That sounded good to me, but I didn't put any sugar in it. That dog sure looked like he was hungry but momma would kill me if I wasted her sugar like that. When he finished shinnin' up the bowl with his tongue, he looked up at me like he wanted more and that's exactly when I named my yellow dog "Biscuit." His big yellow tail started waggin' from side to side and his pink tongue crossed over his

Special Arrangements At Mickey Spitzer's

black lips. I went back in and brought him another bowl of milk and a biscuit broke up in it. I tried to pet him but he kept lickin' my face and barkin' like he was sayin' "Thank you, C.J., thank you; I sure do love you, C.J." He looked real happy to me, he sure did, like he figured he'd finally got exactly to the place where God wanted him to be. I told him he could live with us but Momma would have the last say-so when she got home in just a little while.

When her ride dropped her off and she started walkin' up to the house, she stopped when she saw Biscuit. He was sittin' by me on the steps and started growlin' when he saw Momma. I put my arm around him and told him that was my momma comin' up the road and he would like her. He kept his eyes on Momma as she got closer and closer, and kept on growlin'.

"Hi, Momma," I said to her when she got in talkin' range. "I got me a dog. His name's Biscuit." I could tell she was tired and was gonna have to wash out her white dress and hang it on the line to dry, but Momma was real pretty, the way she walked and the way she fixed up her face and hair, and she had long legs and pretty hands with long fingers. And on Sundays, she was always beautiful for church. "I named him Biscuit, Momma. Ain't that a good name for a yellow dog?"

"Oh, C.J." she said, shaking her head real slow. "I don't know 'bout a dog like Biscuit. He's already big, baby, and he's gonna eat a lot." Her voice was tired, too.

"He's a boy, Momma, look," I said, then told Biscuit to "rollover."

"Yeah," she said. "I can tell, C.J., but right now any dog will be hard for us to take care of," and her lips started quiverin'. "Baby," she said real slow like, "I gotta get Mickey Spitzer's paid off in the next few days before we can get some food, even for us." She smiled a little. "I just don't know, C.J., I just don't know, baby." I thought Momma was gonna cry, but she shook her head and just stood there lookin' at me and then at Biscuit. "But it ain't your place to worry, baby, we'll *get* some groceries." She wiped her eyes with one of those long fingers, then patted Biscuit on his head. She tried real hard to smile, but I saw she just couldn't do it, just like every other time she talked about what we owed at Mickey Spitzer's.

Mickey Spitzer's. I didn't like to go to that store, and I sure didn't like that white man. "Mr. Mickey," Momma said I oughta call him. And anyway, Momma said for me not to go there except with her. His old store was dusty, and hot in the summer and cold in the winter. It was over a mile down the gravel road all the way to the fork, where if you went left, you'd end up in Salem or take the right fork, cross over the old iron bridge, and you'd be in Leggtown. The other store at the fork was Harper's and Momma said they didn't let colored folks have groceries on credit like Mickey Spitzer's.

But anyway, about two weeks after Biscuit came to our house, a bad thing happened. Some logs rolled off a truck at the sawmill and killed Mr. Matson. Miz Matson was Momma's boss lady at the County Home, and the day Mr. Matson died, Momma come home and cried most of the evenin'. She said she needed to do somethin' for her friend and her two little girls. Momma said they had a little bit more than we had, but I didn't know about that, not really, but I sure knew

Special Arrangements At Mickey Spitzer's

Momma worried a lot about our situation. Her hands were shakin' when she told me to go on Friday mornin' down to Mickey Spitzer's while she was at work and get a bag of flour so she could bake a funeral cake for Miz Matson.

Around ten, I tied a piece of twine around Biscuit's neck and we left to walk to Mickey Spitzer's at the fork. I picked up a stick before we got to the Blankenship's, 'cause their old bulldog always come out to the road and got after us every time we went by. With Biscuit by me, I figured that old dog would get real mad when I passed in front of his house. Sure enough, I saw him runnin', little clouds of dust gettin' up behind him. I raised my stick, but he wouldn't stop, and he jumped straight on Biscuit. I hit him with the stick. That still didn't stop him, but when Biscuit bit that bulldog's ear, then his big lip, he yelped and headed back to his yard. Biscuit looked like he was tough, even if he *was* a funny color, and I was proud of what he did. I think he was proud, too.

About then, I saw a car comin', rocks flyin' and dust rollin' in big clouds in back. Biscuit sat at my side on the edge of the ditch till the old car passed. I coughed several times and dusted off my overalls, then wiped Biscuit's face with my hand. He licked my cheek, then we walked on to Mickey Spitzer's.

Just a little ways off, I could see two white men sittin' on Mickey Spitzer's front porch, talkin' and laughin'. When I got closer, I saw 'um leanin' back in their chairs with their arms crossing over their big round bellies, and I recognized old man Moore, the man who comes every month for our rent money. The other old man, I didn't know who he was.

Momma said not to talk like that, "old man so and so," 'specially 'bout a white man we owed rent money to. And I was sorry I said it that way, even to just myself. When we got to the steps, Biscuit saw those two men and wanted to get away. He was scared to death and started pulling real hard on the rope. It almost burned my hand.

"Where'd you git that ole yellow dog you got there, C.J.?" Mr. Moore called to me.

"Well, I'll be!" the other man said real quick. "Boy, you done stole my dog." And then he looked funny at me and asked real mean-like: "What's your name, boy, where you from?" and then he looked hard at Mr. Moore.

"Oh, that's C.J.," Mister Moore told the man, then he laughed and sat up in his chair. "Word is his daddy ran off before C.J. was born, but I'm purty sure there was a white man hidin' in the woodpile, don't you reckon?" Then he looked back at the man and they busted out laughing, like they done lost their minds.

I froze solid when I heard what old man Moore told that man, and before I could tell him how Biscuit showed up at my house, Mr. Mickey walked out the door and his old blue hound jumped down the steps and started smellin' around Biscuit. The hair on Biscuit's back stood straight up and I heard him growl.

"What are you doin' heah, boy?" Mr. Mickey asked me, his face in a pinch.

"That old dog ain't worth a plug nickel," the other old man said real quick. "I'm surprised somebody ain't killed him yet."

I jumped when Mr. Mickey's hound started fightin' Biscuit. I pulled the rope and Mr. Mickey got his dog by his collar and back on the porch then put him inside behind the screen door.

"Darn, boy," Mr. Mickey yelled at me, and I hadn't done a thing bad. "Why in the devil did you come here and bring that dog to my store?"

I didn't know what to say 'bout Biscuit, so I figured I'd tell him why I'd come.

"My momma wants a bag of white flour, to make a funeral cake this evenin'," I called to him. The old man on the porch kept lookin' at Biscuit and me, and mumblin' somethin' to Mr. Moore. Then he spit some tobacco juice in a little can.

In no time, Mr. Mickey walked out the door and handed me a brown paper bag. "You tell your momma that's the last she can have till she makes special arrangements with me. You hear me, C.J.?" I sure didn't know Mr. Mickey knew my name, but he did, and when he handed me that bag, I remembered how Mr. Mickey got real mad one day, the first time I ever heard anything 'bout special arrangements. And that was the day Momma told me to go sit and wait on the porch. I was just a little ole boy then, 'bout five or six I guess.

"Yes, sir, Mr. Mickey," I said and pulled on Biscuit's rope. "I'll tell her what you said." Before I even turned around, Mr. Mickey's old hound come runnin' out the door and jumped on Biscuit, and Mr. Moore and that other old man stood up and started yellin' and cheerin' 'um on. Biscuit and that old dog barked and growled then they rolled together right in front of me, and in no time, blood shot out the hound's neck and he laid down in the rocks at the bottom of the steps, dead as a doornail. Biscuit started smellin' him then backed away and whined, then he leaned against my leg. When I started lookin' close at Biscuit to see if he was hurt any, I heard old man Moore.

"Don't do that, Mickey," he yelled. "Ain't no use in firein' that gun!"

When I looked, Mr. Mickey was standing at the top step, aiming his pistol straight at Biscuit.

"I told you that dog was no good," the other man said. "He's a chicken killer and egg sucker, and oughta be shot."

I heard the gun click, and I looked at Mr. Mickey shakin' like a leaf and sweat runnin' off him like rainwater. That's when I stepped in front of Biscuit.

"Don't do that, Mickey, stop!" Mr. Moore was beggin' Mr. Mickey, and Mr. Moore come down those steps real fast. He grabbed the twine out my hand and at the same time, he shoved me down, flat on my back with the paper sack in my arms. The gun went off and poor Biscuit yelped just one time.

Mr. Mickey yelled somethin' at me, but I didn't stop runnin' till a car caught up with me and I got lost in the dust. The rocks on the road hurt my feet, and the bag of flour got heavy, so I sat under a tree in the ditch and hid behind some Johnson grass, tryin' to figure out what all happened at Mickey Spitzer's. After a little while, I walked on, and there was our house sittin' on a little rise, all gray, and the tin roof was brown and rusty. I knew it was hot in there. Momma said the thermometer hit a hundred the day I was born, and she couldn't remember anybody comin' 'cept old Aunt Alice, a colored lady who births babies for five dollars.

Special Arrangements At Mickey Spitzer's

And Mr. Mickey. Momma said he came after nightfall and delivered two bags of groceries.

When I got to the house, I was sweatin' and didn't wanna go inside. I sat in the shade on the steps and swatted at a couple sweat bees humming around my face. Then I remembered it was Friday, payday, and after we'd bake the funeral cake for Miz Matson, I knew me and Momma would do like we always did on payday—sit on the porch till the sun went down. We'd drink some pop and separate our money. We'd put it in three little bags, one with "rent" marked on it, another one said "lights," and another one said "school for C.J." Every time, Momma would hold up that last little bag and she'd smile, and that's when Momma was the prettiest. And tonight, well I figured we'd talk about Biscuit, and Mr. Mickey, too.

I petted that bag of flour next to me on the steps, right where Biscuit used to sit. I wondered what Momma would say if I told her what old man Moore said to that other white man on Mickey Spitzer's porch. She'd cry. I knew she'd cry. When I thought about what happened to Biscuit, I thought about me, too, and wondered if Momma wouldn't be better off if I just took the other road at the fork and cross over the river, go past Leggtown, and never come back. *No,* I thought, that wouldn't be good, and I figured I'd best tell her what all happened. Momma knew how to get along somehow, 'bout everything, and I sure didn't wanna add to her worries without her knowin' the truth.

I leaned my head against the post, and the katydids got louder, fussin' 'bout the heat, I figured. I closed my eyes, and heck—right inside my head there was Mr. Moore yellin' at Mr. Mickey and the other old white man cussin' Biscuit. And I could see the shine in the barrel of that gun, and Mr. Mickey was sweatin' and frownin' and his face was glowin' white. Well, that's when my eyes just shot wide open, right there on my steps...and the heat looked like water floatin' on the road.

"And anyway, Momma," I said out loud 'cause I wanted to hear it straight through my ears, "we gonna bake a funeral cake as quick as you get home, and Momma," I said, and stopped talkin' completely, jumped up, and yelled "Biscuit!" when I saw him runnin' to me like he was never shot at a-tall. Biscuit just sat there by me and licked the sweat right off my cheeks.

"And tomorrow, Momma," I started over, "we gonna walk down to the fork and tell Mr. Mickey that C.J.'s got Biscuit again, and you got C.J. and glory hallelujah, Momma; I'm tellin' you right now, with a big old boy like C.J., you won't need to make any more special arrangements at Mickey Spitzer's."

A
GOOD
SON

Momma said with no jobs and nothin' to do, made young boys crazy and doll-playin' girls into sweet little mommas way too soon, and she was livin' proof. In the middle of the nights when she cusses Dad, I figure she's lookin' at dreams she didn't wanna see, and when she cries in the dark, it's the name "Mary" she whispers, like Mary's a secret, and I figure she is and likely always will be. The day Momma told Dad we'd have another mouth to feed in a few months, Dad yelled at Momma and tried to hit her, then beat his fist clear through the door, but that don't matter anymore, not at all, 'cause on a cold night when she was two days old, baby Mary stopped breathin'. And the next morning, Dad dug a hole under a pine tree and buried her there in the woods. I helped him. I was about eleven then, and my brother Jay was a bit over two. Ever since, when anything bad happens, Momma brings up Mary's name, cusses Dad, sometimes hits him with whatever is closest or makes his neck bleed with her fingernails, and that's when I know Momma's pain never leaves; just a cruel suffering. And that's when I cut myself with my knife, so I know a little pain, too...just not the kind Momma cries about. Under the pine tree the morning we buried Mary, Dad told Momma that he has to do whatever it takes to stop the ache in our bellies, or get us out the rain... it just don't matter...he says he's gonna do it. And he'll do anything else to help him through the night so to wake up the next mornin' able start all over. I believe him, 'cause that's the way he's done for as long as I can remember.

Last December when I turned fifteen, Momma handed me a fancy cup with a gold stallion on it and soap in it, a round brush with a fancy wooden handle, and a razor with a shiny blade that snapped open. While she held the mirror, she talked about things, about how hard it was to keep on goin', but lucky we had each other. She laughed when I finished cuttin' at my face, and said I was a man and she was proud of me. She said I was a good son, her prince, and was the one who was gonna make things right when I got older…"and you're a beautiful man, like your daddy," she told me, but she said I needed to know "the *truth* about that bastard." I listened, but I didn't know about bein' "beautiful" or bein' a man either; I was just fifteen, and the only grown up man I'd ever been around was my dad, and if I said somethin' like that, Momma would cuss him some more, then say she's "gonna cut his throat one day." And for several years now, I'd seen what all we had to do to get along, and I figured that the truth Momma was talkin' 'bout just didn't matter, none a-tall, and none of us cared anymore…but I'd never hurt my momma by sayin' it to her face.

Even on good days, when Dad would cut up and pick at Momma, trying to bring up her spirits, it looked to me like there wasn't a laugh left inside her to come out. I figured if Dad had any kind of job, Momma might be a little more satisfied, but there weren't any jobs except farm work, but Dad didn't like anything that held him down in one place very long or bein' subject to another man's wants. He was a hard-rock man, but his liquor never got to him, and he proved it every day after the sun went down and still, he was ready the next morning to fight the "whole damn world," is the way he put it. His lanky frame was graceful as a dancer's, Momma said, and his broad shoulders and arms filled up a coat; big hands were strong, and long fingers were as nimble as a fiddle player's. His smile pulled you to him. And you never caught him without his spectacles so "nobody can read me," he'd say. They were round with gold rims; "they have to be real gold," he said, "or they won't work." He's thirty-one years old according to Momma, and a gentleman if the occasion called for it or a strutting "peacock" if any ladies were around to watch him; "full of tricks and a scoundrel straight out of hell," she always added. His name is Richard...Richard Beck.

On New Year's Eve, Dad raised to his lips what was left in a pint of Four Roses instead of moonshine, because it was a special day, the end of 1932, "a lousy year if there ever was one," he said, but we'd been blessed that day when we drove up to an old settler's cabin he remembered in the woods just north of town. It had a decent roof and a fireplace, and was deep enough in the trees, he was sure, that nobody would bother us for several weeks. Later that evening, while firelight shadows danced across the walls, Dad wrapped his arms around Momma, kissed her, and she clung to him, and they slow-waltzed while he sang barely above a whisper: *"Leaning on Jesus, leaning on Jesus, leaning on the everlasting arms."* Momma knew she'd have to get him goin' the next mornin' and name callin' might start all over. But that's when he'd tell her how beautiful she was, how strong and how much he admired her bravery, and how much he loved her, then she'd smile and kiss him.

"And come Easter," Dad said before he laid down on his pallet that night, "good luck was gonna cover us over!" I didn't know how he knew about good luck, or if I'd recognize it if it came, 'cause I'd never been witness to any that I could recall. I figured it was like a lot of other things in Dad's mind, just another wish. And now, Easter is only two days away and we've started a new "run."

In my family, we measure time by the season, only two, summer and winter. I couldn't remember ever stopping long enough to watch spring turn everything green, or fall when everybody had a little money from their crop, because that's when we "ran," were on "excursion." That's what Momma called it…"excursion," a word she saw in an advertisement in the *Athens Democrat*, about the train leavin' Decatur on an "excursion" to Tuscaloosa to a football game. "It was a 'cleaner' word," she said, "more class to it, better than 'run.'"

I'm sittin' on yesterday's *Athens Democrat* right this minute with a headline that tells the whole story: "GAS STOLEN FROM LOCAL STATION." The newspaper said the filling-station man pumped five gallons and the dirty thief drove off before paying a penny, and the sheriff said fifty cents wasn't worth his time to look for the rascal.

Some things I don't know much about seem strange to me, and my own birthday is one of those things. All that Momma ever said was that I was born sometime in December, about the middle. Momma said she remembers it well but claims she don't like birthdays or holidays, except Christmas and Easter, and she likes those because "we stop long enough to think about the Lord, and heaven," and her heaven, she said, "is always white and clean, and glows like fresh snow when the moon is full on a dark, cold night." Dad would smile when she said something about the Lord or heaven, grab her, and they'd dance while he sang a hymn. And Dad said I was born on the railroad platform in Belle Mina, on a cold day, between two bales of cotton left over from the fall, and a colored woman from across the track came over and helped him birth me. Never in my life did I call my dad a liar, but I never believed he gave that woman a whole dollar for her help. And to this day, Dad blames that colored lady for our missing the four o'clock freight down to Hartselle. Momma said we almost froze to death and the trip that night nearly killed both her and me.

Maybe I am a man now, at fifteen, and probably as big as I'll ever be. I've come to like the confidence Momma places in me and I like the responsibility I've carried for a couple of years now. Maybe I ought to start lookin' to go on my own like Momma says. Sometimes I feel like I want to get away, go far away, Kentucky sounded good, even Tennessee...just leave and do the best I can. Still, I figure I need all the learning I can get, and time, if I'm gonna make it.

Ridin' in the back of the truck was cold, the wind whipped around me and cut through my coat. I pulled up the collar tight around my neck and leaned against the side when the truck swerved in the gravel. Rocks flew everywhere. I got a handhold on the side to steady me, and took in a deep breath. The cold air was wet and I could nearly touch the pines right at the sides of the road. Fog in the hollow hid the road behind us. I covered my ears with my hands and cap to warm them and cut out the noise of the rocks slamming under the truck. Sometimes I'd ride for miles with my face in my cap, bracing against the dust, the wind, and the smoke that made my eyes burn.

Since my little brother Jay was big enough to sit on the seat, my place was in back, leaning against the truck cab, with all the boxes and sacks, everything we owned, and we carried it with us most of the time.

The engine backfired, sounded like a gun when Dad shifted gears to slow the truck enough to go down the slope to the landing to get on the ferry and cross the river. The water was green with pools swirling in the middle.

"Been over this river twelve times today," the captain called out. He was old, was stooped; his raincoat long and his hat barely let his eyes show. His voice jerked from loud to soft from word to word, and he coughed just as he flicked his cigarette butt into the water. "Come on now, slow, come on," he ordered, moving his hand so Dad would know to drive the truck over the ramp dropped down from the landin' to the boat. "And this is 'bout the last crossin' till after Easter. You folks just made it," he said. Momma handed him some money through the window. A couple minutes later, another man hollered at two mules, their long ears drooping almost to their blinders, then clicked his tongue till the ferry moved away from the bank to take us across Elk River.

On the other side, the truck struggled to climb from the ferry up to a flat spot then stopped. Momma left my little brother Jay on the seat next to Dad. Jay stared in front. He was pale and still weak from the fever he'd caught last summer when we lived in the woods on the river close to Paint

Rock. "Push," Momma said, sounding half-mad. "Push, Prince!" The truck motor rattled like rocks in a tin bucket, and blue smoke shot out the pipe in back. We pushed till the truck climbed up the bank onto the gravel road. A raindrop hit my cheek and the breeze was cold, comin' from the north. Momma wrapped her arms around herself and looked at me with a half-smile.

"You done good, Prince," she said and stood on tiptoes to kiss my cheek. My nose filled with the smell of sandalwood, a "cover-up" Momma called it, for when she didn't have a place or time to bathe and clean up.

Dad's name is Richard and mine, too. Momma said we were alike in name first, then in our stature and the way we carried ourselves, and on a dark night, she couldn't tell the difference between us. She said we swaggered on long legs, looking like boys who'd played all day with *Jack Daniel*, then she'd laugh, "but more than any other way," she always added, "y'all prance like kings, like you own the whole damn world." During times when she cursed at life itself or times she wanted to kill Dad, Momma called him "King" and if her anger grew to fist blows, she called him "King Richard" and if her anger got big and rowdy, it filtered down to me and she called me "Prince." And for some time now, right before Easter, her name callin' had taken over.

"Y'all git in the damn truck, you two," Dad yelled. When I glanced, Momma's freckles had spread, making her face one color; her auburn hair was pulled up and pinned in curls high on her head, her frilly white dress from a "poor box" we found somewhere hung below her knees. She was as beautiful as any girl in the magazines we looked at in the drug store in town, and sometimes, she seemed no more real than the doll she hid in her sack of clothes since the day Dad buried baby Mary in the woods. Right then, Momma stood as still as a statue with eyes set, looking across wide-open land, where rainwater sat in little pools, where the river spilled over when it rained too much. My eyes followed hers as she looked at the lay of the land and how it rose naturally, but barren and wet with leftover winter.

"This is poor country, Prince," she said while shaking her head with despair locked on her face. "There's not much here to help us along, just dirt and rocks is all I see. Nature's poor here…real poor," and her voice died away. She whipped around, gathered the hem of her dress in one hand, and climbed into the truck. Jay took his place on her lap. I jumped to my seat in back and sat on newspaper, then pulled my collar tight around my neck. Over the flat land, a hundred yards from the road, stood a big white house with several tall graveyard trees in front. It was alone, lonely, at the top of the rise, and dark smoke came out of a chimney. The house was the only thing in all directions that showed there might be life anywhere around, and in back of the big house, in the distance, was a curtain of low hills, smoky and blue. *Tennessee*, I thought, remembering the picture calendar one of Dad's cousins from Tennessee gave us a couple years ago. And I figured this "excursion" was gonna be a new adventure, and summer would probably be spent roaming those blue hills or in an old shack in the woods, not far from a little town nestled in a valley those hills made. As far as I knew, we'd never gone more than fifty miles in any direction from Limestone County, or crossed the line out of Alabama, but those far-off hills took on the look of an invitation for a new beginning, a different life, maybe even a job, to work for cash money, maybe a home to live in. I looked again at the white house.

I was cold all the way through, and I had to grab the side again to hold on. A lump came in my throat and I wanted to cry for me and cry for my family, but when I thought about those blue hills, I became anxious, wishing we wouldn't stop, just keep goin' far away, till we found a place somewhere in those hills.

Without any words said, I knew that on this excursion, like so many others, we were slipping through the fingers of the sheriff, and this time, for five gallons of gas. Momma had already come to name callin', and threats for starting another excursion so soon, but like other times, she'd get over it after a little while and become excited by the "run" itself, and settlin' in a new spot where everybody was a stranger and nobody knew our name.

I slammed against the side when the truck swerved in the gravel as it turned onto a narrow road goin' uphill, then turned again to climb farther into the woods. A couple minutes later, we came to a clearing with winter-dead grass up to my chest, and surrounded on three sides by tall pines, their tops swaying and moaning in the steady breeze out the north.

The brakes squeaked for a second and the truck came to a stop at the front porch of an old house, gray, and worn ragged by time and nature, its chimney and rooftop covered with a vine already green and a few orange flowers, shivering in the cold breeze.

My cap and face were wet. I jumped from the truck, stood on the porch, and looked around while I shook off the wetness.

"I know this old place," Dad said, glancing around as he stepped onto the porch, a smile crossing his face. "I used to hunt up here. These hills belonged to old man Cain, and I'd hunt all over his place." Dad ran his fingers through his thick hair, and his smile grew bigger. "Man, I kept that old bastard runnin', tryin' to catch me on his land...Sam Cain's place." He shook his head then pressed his finger to the center and pushed up his glasses, his eyes blinked. "People used to say the government gave his daddy these good-for-nothin' goat hills right after they shipped all the Indians to Oklahoma." Dad kicked the half-opened door and laughed. "And who'd ever believe it's gonna be mine for a while." He grabbed my shoulder with his big hand and shook me. "Richard, boy, go help your Momma unload the truck before everything gits wet. I'm gonna git some wood to warm up this place."

A few minutes later, the four of us stood watching the fire grow into tall orange flames, lighting the dark room, and our hands reaching to the warmth. In the middle of the room, everything we owned was in four boxes and six croaker sacks and a canvas bag holding a tin box that only Momma ever looked in.

On one side of the room were two straight chairs and a small table leftover from somebody else, and on the front wall, dim daylight showed through cracks as wide as a man's finger. I checked the latch on the front door, then opened it to look at the trees and rain, and jumped when two raccoons

A Good Son

shot through the door from the dark room to the right. Momma screamed and grabbed for my brother. "Damn," Dad yelled, "but that's all right. This has probably been their home long before we got here. We just gotta clean it up a little and it's gonna be fine and dandy." Dad kept "fine and dandy" on the tip of his tongue.

Momma rested her hands on her hips and watched as Jay backed up to the fire, his arms hanging down and hands clasped together in back. My little brother was ragged; his cloths were like mine, tattered in the collar, and pants with busted-out knees, clothes passed to us by gray-haired church ladies who never asked us where we lived.

"Help me with these blankets and quilts," Momma said as she leaned over the sacks in the middle of the room. "Tomorrow we'll clean up the dust and spider webs, get this place lookin' like home." She always said something like that, but I really didn't know what she meant...maybe there was a time when she had a home, maybe when she lived with her people on a farm down on the Warrior River, but I figured "home" was a fantasy that she wouldn't give up. She had other fantasies, about Dad, some about me, some I figured I'd try to meet as best I could for Momma's sake. Dad said they were dreams, but maybe there was a home when Dad had work, maybe before hard times took over our lives, but I never knew us when we had a "home." But, "home" was a good word, a warm word, like hope and love. I wished I could say "home" as easily as Momma did, but I couldn't... all I could do was guess about what that word meant. Standing over those sacks and boxes, Momma's freckles had left and her face looked happy, and under that mask, I knew there was a woman with a powerful mind that showed through her personality and what she did for her family. She always knew what the next step was, how to "get by," and she knew how to do whatever it took to make life work.

Dad pulled up a straight chair to the fire, took out a bag of Bull Durham from his coat pocket, and rolled a cigarette. Smoke came out of him in a cloud, a soft blue haziness between the dark where I stood and the firelight on the other side of where he sat. Mostly, Dad had little to say, and that night, with a creased forehead and his eyes wandering through the room, he pressed his hands to his face. He was lost in his thoughts, I figured, and wondered what to do for his family. Momma said he'd lost his soul to hard times a long while back, but his pride was still there, and could never be snatched from him. I wondered what Dad was thinking just then, what was going through his mind. He glanced at me and Momma then took in a deep breath of Bull Durham smoke and let it out, and when he saw me watching him, he smiled, a weak smile, I was sure to cover the shame of hiding his family in another man's house.

"Over there," Momma said, pointing to a corner. "Put your and Jay's bed there, Prince. And you gonna need plenty of cover before mornin'." She opened a paper sack and looked inside, then pulled out several potatoes and an onion. "Not much," she said, shaking her head. "King Richard, you need to find us a rabbit out here, or somethin'. We need some food." Her knuckles showed white on the hand that grasped the sack. "You hear me, Richard...you hear me, King?"

"I hear you, darlin'; yeah, I heard what you said," he answered in a soft voice, never taking his eyes from the fire.

My hearing Dad's real name "Richard" from Momma's lips made me figure that this crumbling little shack, a place to live in for a little while, had eased the anger that seemed always boiling between them. And that was good.

For supper, Momma cooked the potatoes with the onion in a heavy black pot on top of the fire, and later, she found a bunch of broken-up cookies in her coat pocket, cookies I'd lifted from a grocery store a few days before. After a while, Jay fell asleep on the pallet, the fire died to small yellow flames and red coals, and I laid almost asleep next to my little brother on the floor in the corner.

"No, Richard, not now," Momma whispered in the quiet dark. Dad mumbled something and then several scratches came from the front wall under the porch. Dad shot up and scrambled for his Mauser, then listened with one ear against the door.

"Those damn raccoons wanna git back in," he said, and moved slowly through the dark back to a pallet of quilts and blankets. The red coals in the fireplace were almost gone. I closed my eyes and pulled the cover over my ears because I knew what was coming.

Unable to hold back, I heard Momma whispering and Dad softly grunting, and after a few minutes, he took in a deep breath and held it for a second and then sighed softly. It had always been those times between them, even during long periods when over and over, Momma screamed Mary's name, and she'd call Dad nothing but "King Richard." Jay was far too young to know or question, but a long time back I came to understand and accept their times of lovemaking, after which, it seemed, there might be several days of peace between them. Tomorrow, I was sure now, was going to be a better day, far less name-calling and fewer flares of aggravated temper.

The next morning on the front porch, I found several sticks of wood Dad had gathered and wads of sage grass for lighting a fire. I brought it in and seconds later, the wood had caught and I went back outside. The sun was showing over the blue hills in the east, and from the cabin porch, I found the big white house nestled in the cold shadows about a mile away and studied it. Again, blue smoke was curling upward but was lost quickly in the glaring sunshine. I checked out our truck and then walked down the path and found a spring flowing sweet, clear water from a rock ledge. I ran back to the cabin and got the bucket. Momma would be happy for the fresh water, to drink and to cook with, and to wipe the dust and spider webs from our newfound home. Back on the porch, I stopped and studied the white house again, looking for life around it, any movement at all, and there was none.

"Let her rest, Richard," Dad whispered when I set the bucket of water on the table. He smelled his shirt, dropped it on the floor, then reached in his sack for a clean one and finished dressing. That morning when I heard my name, I knew I'd guessed right during the night...a sweeter day had come. Dad put on his long coat. "I'm goin' back toward the river for a little while," he whispered. "See if you can trap a rabbit or squirrel, and get it ready for her to cook for dinner, and you'll have to find some wood." After a few minutes, I heard the truck start up and its familiar sounds slowly died in the trees.

By two o'clock, Momma, Jay, and I had finished eating a duck I'd caught in my trap at the spring, and we had cleaned up the inside of the cabin. We moved the straight chairs onto the porch, wrapped ourselves in blankets, and listened for Dad's truck to come up the trail through the woods. Momma wouldn't talk and Jay sat on her lap, pulling his hair till he had nearly a handful curling through his fingers. I got him from Momma and held him while he cried softly. I told him everything was okay, I loved him, and I was glad he was my little brother.

"That bastard," Momma finally spoke. "No telling what he's gonna get into, get hisself hurt or get in trouble, and here we are hiding on the side of a hill in this cold jungle." The sun had left us again, and drops of rain blew in onto the porch. Back in the cabin, I relit the fire and held Jay till he went to sleep, then I laid him on the pallet of quilts. Momma's eyes locked to mine when the hum of a motor came from the front of the cabin. The sounds were different, and in an instant, fear twisted Momma's face. She moved quickly to the door, swung it open, and stood with her hands on her hips. I stood behind her, looking over her shoulder. She stepped through the door onto the porch; I moved beside her. "Stay still, Prince," she said softly, and slipped her hand into a jacket pocket, checking for Dad's old Mauser, and then crossed her arms in front, hiding the pistol in the fold of her elbow. She waited.

"My name is Samuel Cain." A big man in a long raincoat and bushy, gray eyebrows spoke slowly in a bellowing voice while he stood at the door of our truck, and in one hand, he held a shotgun, pointed toward Momma. She didn't move.

"I believe this is your man, ma'am, and I've killed him." He glanced at me then back to Momma. The rain had stopped but the breeze was cold. I heard Momma breathe deeply then her chest rose and fell as her breaths came faster. She cupped one hand over her mouth. Samuel Cain glanced into the back of the truck, then reset his eyes on Momma.

"Go see, Prince," she said softly, "it can't be so, but see what it's about." I stepped from the porch and Mr. Cain quickly raised his gun, pointing it to my chest. I locked my eyes on his, and walked straight toward him.

"Is that your daddy, boy?" he asked. Another man waited in another truck in back of ours.

"Yes," I said. I looked at Dad lying cheek-down on the wet truck bed, his back speckled where buck shot had peppered through his canvas coat. I heard Momma whimpering. "Why?" I asked, my words rushed out and I glared in the man's face: "What the hell did he do that said you had to *kill* him?" Momma came to the truck, both hands covering her nose and mouth, hiding what she felt.

"He broke into my larder and stole my food. I didn't mean to kill him, but it happened," Mr. Cain said.

"Where's his hat and glasses?" I asked. Momma had moved beside me. Her eyes were open wide, glaring at Dad.

"Right here," he said and held out a burlap sack weighted heavily with something inside. "There's a twenty-pound ham and other food he took. He's paid an awful price for it, so I guess it's yours now. And what's his name?" Mr. Cain asked.

"Ralph," I replied quickly. "His name is Ralph Smith." I leaned closer over Dad, pressed my hand onto his forehead,

A Good Son

and in my mind, everything sharpened, became clear when I raised his eyelid and his eye turned up to me. I reached for the sack Mr. Cain held with one hand while he pointed his gun toward me. I stood between the big man and Momma; she folded her fingers and soothed Dad's brow with the back of her hand. She cut her eyes up to me, squinted, then let her knees fold. She knelt on the ground beside me and wept, hiding her face in her hands.

"And you shot him in the back," I said, and spat on the ground at Mr. Cain's feet, then glared in his face.

"He was runnin', boy, runnin' like thieves do," Mr. Cain said, almost shouting. He hesitated for a second. "And when the ferry starts up on Monday, y'all take the body to town and report to the sheriff. He'll get to my place after noon some time, and I'll tell him my side of what happened."

Momma's hands folded in prayer and her words bounced around in my head. "Lord, Lord, Lord," she said, and silently, I said the words she prayed. "What in the world am I gonna do, no husband and no place to live with two kids to raise?" I had heard her prayer several times, and as far as I knew, it was ever-going, and the Lord had no need to be roused by Momma's question. Again, she covered her face with both hands and her body jerked with silent weeping. When Mr. Cain rustled his raincoat, Momma frowned and cut her eyes up to him. He reached into the coat and pulled out a small black purse.

"I own this place and this little ole cabin, and I'm gonna let y'all stay here at least for a while. There's plenty to eat in these woods, good water and a lake full of fish," With my eyes locked on him, Mr. Cain nodded toward me. "And you got another man here...looks like he already knows how to carry on." He snapped open the purse and dumped everything on the ground at Momma's knees. "That's more than enough to bury this scoundrel, and enough to help y'all along till y'all find a place to light in," he said. "Now, boy," he nodded with his overgrown eyebrows pointing to Dad, "what do you reckon to do with this body till Monday?"

"Just keep your damn hands off him," I said quickly, squinting and glaring into the old man's eyes. "I can take care of him; it's cold enough on the porch."

Mr. Cain shook his head as he walked away, then turned and pointed his finger at Momma. "You're just a bunch of drifters...just good-for-nothin' drifters is all," he said. "And your man got what he deserved; just sorry I'm the one who did it." He got in his truck and slammed the door. The sound of the engine died away as the truck moved into the woods.

We watched from the cabin porch till the truck came out of the woods, crossed the highway, and became a speck at the front of the white house. Thin blue smoke from a chimney was moving slowly in waves down the slope toward the river.

We celebrated, and tomorrow we'd celebrate again... Easter Sunday...a holiday Momma liked. Thin sunshine cut the chill, the breeze was cold but sweet, and King Richard was yet to say anything about his and our accomplishments. He leaned against a post, struck a match, and lit a cigarette, the whole time his eyes set on Mr. Cairn's big white house, and a telling grin crossed his face. Already, on the front porch of the cabin, out of Mr. Cain's twenty-pound ham, I had plucked enough buckshot, and said out loud: "Plenty enough to kill a regular man, but..."

"But *not* King Richard," Momma cut in quickly, smiling, and she leaned against me, her eyes looking up to my face. I took in a faint new-washed smell, the aroma of flowers from her body and dress. She was beautiful, and I saw a glow of pride in her eyes and on her face as she glanced from me back to Dad. Then her smile became fragile. But I wasn't gonna say what Momma said about Dad. I wanted to tell her I could feel everything I'd ever learned when I saw Dad's eyes with his cheek pressing the floor of the truck; I knew what I had to do then, and I had no fear. I wanted to tell her she was right...I am a man and I'm ready to stand alone, ready to pull my weight. When I looked again at Momma, her eyes glistened with wetness. She shook her head.

"You're a good son, and you're my prince, but you have to get the hell out of here before another generation like this one starts up." Her lips quivered. She took my hand, and in it, she placed a Bull Durham bag with a roll of cash inside. "And don't look back," she said softly, as a tear slid down her cheek.

I looked at Dad. Without his glasses, I read his eyes and his face without his smile. He pushed his cap back and sighed, watched Momma closely and saw her tears, too, then shook his head. He didn't have to say a word when his eyes latched onto mine, and I knew his thoughts as his eyes shifted to the big white house a mile down the hill. Then he danced passed me to Momma, and slipped a Bull Durham bag of tobacco and matches into my coat pocket. His long body straightened up and his arms spread wide as he moved, then he wrapped his arms around her, kissed her and began to sway. He kissed her again with both big hands caressing her cheeks, and hummed. The tune came to me and seeing their dance, I smiled and mouthed the words: *"Amazing Grace, how sweet the sound that saved a wretch like me..."* Their movements became passionate, and I knew their night would also be.

Leaving was our nature, the way we did things, and saying good-bye was never part of leaving. In the early morning dark, I put on my coat and picked up my sack of belongings. I walked down the slope through the woods, watching my white breaths explode in front of me, while the tall pines with black trunks stood at attention like soldiers shivering in icy-white cold. A deep frost covered the ground. *Easter Sunday,* I remembered, and figured by the time the sun would light the cabin, Jay would have a fire going and would fetch a bucket of fresh water, his jobs now with Momma's help... he'd learn to read her voice and learn from the experiences of a loving mother. I thought about her beauty, her power, the love for her children, and about her frequent advice... and how I'd let her words run off me like rainwater. *This time is different,* I thought, *and maybe the last time I'll ever hear her advice, or her voice, but I have to do what I know to make my way, to get along.*

I left the dark woods; the hairs made my arms tingle, while I glared at Mr. Cain's big house frozen in whiteness, as white and clean as what Momma had always said heaven would be like. I looked south, to the flat land sliding into a deep fog, standing solid like a forbidding white wall hiding the dirt, the rocks, and the river. I looked again at "heaven" and hated it, because I knew it was a dream way too big and too far away for a person like me, for people like my family, "a bunch of good-for-nothin' drifters," as old man Cain had said to my mother.

My heart pounded in the ends of my fingers.

I didn't know if things would be better or worse for my family, or for me, but for certain, I would do whatever I had to do to get along, and figured there was no better way to start my first excursion than with Mr. Samuel Cain. I crossed the road and moved slowly through the dim light along the fencerow of brush and small trees, gathering a handful of sage grass as I walked. I glanced back to the hill where smoke was blooming from the cabin chimney, and smiled, knowing that this was a day after one of their nights of lovemaking and Momma would be happiest, even forgiving, and Dad would hold her in his arms and slow-dance while he sang a hymn about Jesus.

From the Bull Durham bag in my pocket, I pulled a match and lit the sage grass, then threw it under "heaven"... "for us drifters, Mr. Cain," I whispered softly..."for my mother, Mr. Cain, you son of a bitch."

I shook with cold as the first rays of the sun appeared over the faraway hills in front of me, turning the sky into a raging, fiery, orange sea—the light of a new beginning, the start of *my* life, who I was. I turned and looked back over the rolling hills at the flames rising above the trees as heaven burned, and I knew Dad would be proud when he saw it. I also knew he'd never tell Momma the truth about her baby, Mary—that it was her good son, her Prince who had smothered Mary under a pile of quilts.

THE ENCHANTING DR. MARQUISE AND RHETT

The four black women are singers and the three white women with blue hair and books always arrive about the same time, faithfully, every Wednesday at two, the time when I meet my new patient. The singers take their music to the dining room, practicing, I was told, for Sunday choir at Mount Zion Baptist Church right up the road a ways, while the three white women wander from room to room handing out tracts and readin' the Bible to anybody who didn't want to listen to the way those black women sang hymns.

Following Mrs. Sabatini's fast gait, I stepped around people going in all directions and a couple of wheelchairs with old ladies in them. In the first one, Mrs. Beverly was sleeping, out cold and her head tilted to the side as drool seeped onto her bib where several spots of lunch had dried. Mrs. Betty Jean was in the second wheelchair. She looked up, smiling and queen-like, she extended her hand as though she expected I'd bow and kiss it. Poor old soul, she'll never understand there are no queens around this place. I started to tell her that, and suggest she stop pretending, but it wouldn't have done any good. And somebody had made up her face with all good intentions, but to me she looked like a clown straight out of the circus I went to when I was little, or maybe she *was* a clown forty years back. Who knows the stories about all these old people...and it looks like to me that there's nobody to listen anyway. *No,* I thought, *Mrs. Betty Jean's much too old to remember anything or who she was a long time ago, but I could have told her I liked her hair,* which was a telltale sign of a woman come in from a different time zone. "Hey, Doctor," she said as I approached her, then her eyes drifted aimlessly somewhere down the hall. "Hello, good-lookin', hello good-lookin', you wanna dance, honey, it's just a dime?" she asked, then asked again and kept asking till I was thirty feet past, and then her crackly voice just died away in the everyday sounds bouncing up and down the hall.

But I was glad every time a new patient came to live at Sunny Acres...I could care for them the same as I'd done for quite a while now. I liked the administrator and he never complained about me, so he must have thought I was a good doctor, and besides, it wasn't easy to find a young doctor who wanted to take care of all these old folks. Who knows why is anybody's guess, but I'd heard Nurse Sabatini complain that a doctor couldn't build his future on old people because old people just didn't last very long. But anyway, I know everybody loves me, mostly because I give them plenty of time to tell me their problems...and I listen to their stories if they can remember...and I hear other crap, too, if they want to talk about it.

I was almost in a run behind Sabatini. "Room twenty-two north," she said, mostly to herself while she knocked softly on a door with two big *twos* in the middle. She cracked the door a little. "Celeste?" she said with a question in her tone, as though she wasn't sure if the new patient was there or not. I leaned against the handrail in the hall to wait while

Nurse Sabatini welcomed Celeste and tell her a few of the rules at Sunny Acres. When she finished with the rules, I heard her clearly. "Celeste, your doctor will be here shortly, darlin', just a routine first visit. His name is Doctor Marquise." That was my queue, and I was ready to impress the new lady...I cleared my throat and checked my white jacket for red spots, remembering we'd had spaghetti a couple days ago.

"Oh," the new lady said, just as I glanced into the room. She had looked up from the book she held with both hands, making me figure those blue-haired ladies had gotten there first, but it wasn't the Bible she had latched on to. I ducked back and waited outside the door, preferring to make a grand entrance like an actor's first appearance onto a stage.

"That's a nice name for a doctor, classy to say the least," Celeste said to Nurse Sabatini, and I thought immediately, *Wow, this one I could tell already was going to be a challenge.* I peeked through the door again, just as Celeste primped her hair with her long fingers, her nails bright red, and then she continued: "By the way, Mrs. Sabatini...I'm up in years, sweetpea, but I'm not deaf, and in case you've forgotten... my name is Mrs. Segers." She held "Segers" for three or four seconds while forcing a smile, then her eyes squinted as daggers flew straight at Sabatini. When Nurse Sabatini passed me, I could tell she was steaming after a put-down like that, but like all the nurses I knew, Sabatini was an expert at holding in her disgust, and for me personally, that was a blessing. As she pranced down the hall mumbling under her breath, I decided I'd go on in and get things going with my new patient in room twenty-two north. I stepped into the room and cut a big smile for Mrs. Segers, hoping she'd recall "Rhett Butler."

"Good afternoon, Doctor Marquise. Thank you for taking my case," Celeste said sweetly, and I smiled with a special curve in my lips, similar to Rhett's when he told Scarlet he really didn't give a damn. Standing beside her bed, I smelled the Jergens, my favorite lotion of all time, the same as my mother used when I was little. Already, I *liked* this lady.

"Oh, I'm delighted to be your doctor, Mrs. Segers," I said, hoping to sound grateful and appreciative as though I really needed another patient, but I could tell that Mrs. Segers was a breath of freshness in the usually tepid air of the nursing home, like sunshine compared to most of the other eighty patients for which I felt responsible. Immediately, I was *taken* with her alertness and how admiringly she looked at me.

Big, round, black-rimmed glasses made her eyes appear larger, and brought out the fine wrinkles of crow's feet at their sides, a sign of intelligence, I believe. Her salt-and-pepper hair, mostly salt, was cut short, was free to blow, and I was sure, the style in which she had worn it for most of her life. She looked comfortable, and her makeup was well done. A mannerism with her hand and lips was a little sensuous for Sunny Acres, I thought, and she reminded me of a woman who tended bar at Zero's Palace on Bourbon Street. But most impressive was what I recognized as power; already she had shot holes through Nurse Sabatini, and I really liked that. I smiled at this sweet, elegant woman, because, I suppose, she made it plain that she needed me, and that made my job a lot easier. I was pleased, too.

"Well, Mrs. Segers," I said, "you and I are going to be good friends, I can tell."

"That's my plan, also, Dr. Marquise," she said, smiling. It was obvious that Mrs. Segers was becoming as giddy as a homecoming queen at halftime on a Friday night. Her smile was cute and she cut her eyes to mine. "And I expect no miracles, only loving understanding for an old woman who has seen her day." *Heck!* I thought, *I prefer homecoming queen over old woman.* She chuckled, "I'm just an old broad with a mission to complete before her time runs out." Then she smiled, tilted her head slightly, and her eyes sparkled. She was back to being a homecoming queen, and I smiled back.

But I figured the conversation was getting a little ambiguous, quickly, too, and a little deep, possibly beyond what was expected of me in the doctor-patient relationship thing. Some details I didn't care to know about a patient anyway, and besides, most had lived far longer than I and had done a lot more things. Sometimes I felt diminished, and that was bad when I did.

Darn! Sabatini had given me an old stethoscope, a broken one, but I pretended to hear anyway. Then I thumped on her back. That startled her, and when I looked, her eyes were tremendous behind her glasses. She squeaked something, then quickly pulled her gown up to her neck, afraid, I suppose, that with my looking down the way I was doing, I might see her boobs. "Date of birth, please?" I asked quickly, and smiled the finest Rhett Butler I'd ever done, after seeing her boobs were just long, pink sacks. Poor lady.

"June twenty-sixth, 1946," she said, then spoke softly, directly to me, as though I were her closest friend. "I'm here, dear boy," she said. She hesitated for a second, then her eyes turned up to me again, unblinking through those big glasses; "I gave up something of myself a long time ago, and I'm hoping you're willing to help me."

Her tone was sweet but her words didn't make sense, so I was sure then that I'd underestimated the degree of confusion in this frisky little lady.

"We'll see about that, Mrs. Segers," I said kindly, in Rhett's best doctor voice. "We'll have to work on it, I guess; in fact, I'm pretty sure we can get together on something."

"Well," she said, smiling, "I made a plan a long time ago, and I've worked my plan for many years, but now, I find that time is running out *for me*." I pulled the chair closer to the bed and sat down, trying my best to show understanding, kindness, and patience.

"When I was twelve, my mother suddenly died of heart failure," she said. "...she was very young, and I knew it wasn't her heart that killed her, Dr. Marquise." *Wow,* I thought, *that was a quick start, and a mystery story to boot.* "In a drunken stupor, my father hit her, hit her several times. Unfortunately, back then, the authorities didn't really investigate as closely as they do today." *Huh,* I thought, *investigate...a word like that strikes fear into doctors, even Sunny Acres' administrator...*and besides, I wasn't into old mysteries with anyone at Sunny Acres. "Nevertheless," the old lady continued, "I was left in a state of helplessness and fear with no one to turn to for help." Her chin rose and her eyes brightened. *Good,* I thought again, *maybe she likes the way my face takes on the Rhett Butler "I know everything" look when I squint my eyes and listen closely with my lips in a half-smile. I need a mustache.*

Suddenly I realized time was flying, and I wondered if it was wise that I spend so much of my time listening to this woman spout off about old times, and in all probability, the more she talked, the more confused she'd become. And what she'd said was becoming far out. Maybe this was the moment to flat out tell her, "Frankly, my dear, I don't give a damn." I sighed, figuring Rhett would use that little gem later, so I held back.

"By the time I was fourteen, I'd become an accomplished thief, stealing what I wanted from food stores and department stores up and down Canal Street." She chuckled. "That's how I got my first pair of high-heel shoes, red ones, and I had to hide them from my father or he would have cursed for two days then would have thrown them away."

"Why did you do that, Mrs. Segers, resort to thievery?" I asked, feeling sure she'd be unable to correlate to reality, but I found her story to be interesting, especially imagining her walking around in red, high-heel shoes, just the shoes. Wow! The hair on my arms stood up.

"Well, I felt I was entitled to whatever my heart desired, Dr. Marquise," she said, her shoulders rose as her voice went higher. She sighed. "I suppose because my mother had been taken away and I was left with a drunk for a father, and he disliked me as much as I disliked him." Her voice was rising again, became shrill, and pins were piercing my eardrums. "Besides, I enjoyed the adrenalin rush when I stole," she said. *Oh*, I thought, *that's it. She enjoyed it. Uh huh, she's a born thief, and everybody around here will be missing their new gowns, toothpaste, and styling gel, and Nurse Sabatini needs to know.*

"Well, I can understand how you might have felt, Mrs. Segers." I said, and sort of laughed, remembering the adrenalin rush when I stole candy or bubble gum from the corner gas station in my old neighborhood. *But what the heck, I thought, leave old Sabatini on her own about Mrs. Segers being a crook. I like this lady better than Sabatini, anyway.* She fingered a tear in her eye, and I wondered where we were going in her story.

"To escape from my father, at seventeen, I quit school and found a job in a touristy bar on Esplanade Avenue. That's where I met a boat captain who had piloted barges up and down the Mississippi for twenty years, and we married." Her eyes became watery. *Oh, now she's gonna tell me about how she stole whiskey and money out the cash register,* I thought. "Dr. Marquise, the captain was a kind man and always neat as a pin in his white shirt and blue trousers, and a blue cap he wore as a badge of distinction and authority. Bless his heart…he thought of me as a *port* convenience." *Sex again, poor lady…the same over and over, just like all the others.* "But the captain was super intelligent, and for that fact, I was thankful, because by the second month into our marriage, I was expecting a child, and I already knew I was going to leave the captain."

I sighed and was sure I wanted to hear more after sex had become rampant in her story, the eventual subject just about every time I visited one of the other old ladies. When I thought about it, I figured it was the Rhett Butler syndrome they loved. But I wondered how I would handle it if her problem continued along sexual lines. I was sure Rhett would know how to deal with it, but right then, I didn't have the time to figure it out. Somewhat pleadingly, I said: "Mrs. Segers, please, my time is limited."

She gasped. "So is mine, Doctor, so is mine," she said, placing her hand on her really flat chest where bosoms usually are. Her face was in surprise mode and her head tilted to the side. Behind the glasses, her eyes demanded my attention. "You should know these things, certainly for my sake but for yours also...for medical analysis, young man." Her voice tipped up as she spoke. "It's important, Doctor, that you document medical history, you know."

Uncertainty had stepped in, I felt it, and I was sorry my comment had put some of it there, but I could tell she longed for my attention and was far more demanding than the typical patient. But still, I couldn't figure out why her story weighed so heavily on me, making me curious and wanting to hear it, all of it.

"Well, I have a few minutes more," I said, and smiled a concession, like Rhett would have done, and posed my eyes just perfectly, so she'd think I awaited her next sensuous move. I shook my head and sighed, knowing also I was committing to listening to her as long as her heart desired. But on the other hand, I knew that would please her.

"Thank you, Dr. Marquise. You're as kind as what I would have expected and I thank you so very much," she said as her eyes brightened. While waiting a couple seconds, she adjusted her gown and neatly folded the sheet after pulling it up to her chin. Her black-rim glasses sat on the tip of her nose. "Well, it was 1963 when I had a fine baby, beautiful and healthy, and I put the child in the hands of the nuns who ran Charity Hospital. They had been kind to me and assured me there was heartfelt justice for my baby, for me, and for the mother who would rear the child as her own. They also assured me my baby would go to a wonderful family right here in New Orleans."

With a tissue, she blotted tears from her cheeks, streaking the makeup, uncovering the yellowish skin, a telltale sign of something really bad.

"A year or so later," she continued, "I asked a few friends for money, figuring some would happily donate just to get me out of their lives, and I boarded a flight to San Diego, California, a place I'd read about, a place where nobody knew me, where I could start over. I intended to paint over the terrible colors of the life I'd lived, and I started with schooling, then honorable work, and I became a new person." Tears nestled in her eyes this time and she made no effort to wipe them away. I was impressed and sympathetic, but I was sure Rhett wouldn't give in at this point, fall apart, and let Scarlett see him cry.

At this time in Mrs. Segers's story, the desire for me to "move on" was abandoned, and I felt I'd given in already to *listening without a choice,* like a third grader having to listen to his teacher read another story about Lassie. She coughed lightly, and then held her hand to her forehead.

"My, my, my," she said, shaking her head as her eyes rolled upward. "Remembering is getting to be a chore, Doctor, but I've discovered a most rewarding pastime—exciting and lively, finding the memories that justify conversations like this one." She smiled and reached toward me, so I moved my hand for her to touch. "Thank you, dear boy," she said, and lovingly patted my hand.

She continued. "I finished college in the spring of 1969 and found work quickly at the Naval Air Station...a wonderful job with marvelous people around me, and it was there I met Lieutenant John Segers, a beautiful young man, a pilot...a graduate of the Naval Academy, and we married in June of the next year." Mrs. Segers glanced through the window, then quickly back to me. "I know you're too young to remember that horrible war, the Vietnam War. It was raging then, halfway around the world, and John flew twenty-three missions over those jungles, and he refused to talk about it when he came home on leave. Poor boy...all he'd say was he was the luckiest man alive...he wasn't among the thousands dying there, and he had me to come home to...what a sweet way he chose to express his love."

I, too, thought that was nice, but I had begun to lose interest until, again, she brought sex back into the story. She spread her thin fingers then, and with her other hand, she played with her gold wedding band, almost spinning it on her skinny finger. She was in pain. She looked up at me. "After all the warring anyone could imagine, and the horror and terror John had been through, he made it home when the war ended in 1973. The next four years were happy for us, then around ten o'clock one morning, I was called by the police who told me John had been in a terrible car crash on the freeway, only five miles from home." She shook her head. "Then, of course, my life took another turn when John died...John died, ending his own suffering...death being the healer, stopping the flow of bloody memories of a terrible war that had taken over his mind...poor, sweet John." She looked through the window to the clouds outside. "He was a soldier, a fighter, but was never a killer. John was an example of a man who served honorably and willingly when his country called." Her voice was low by then, but solid and her words distinct, like Scarlet had done when she clenched her fists in the cornfield, vowing she'd never let her family be hungry again. I couldn't help that a tear came to my eye then.

I wanted to squeeze Mrs. Segers's hand, console her, and tell her how sorry I was for so many unfortunate circumstances in her life, but I couldn't. With everything I was hearing, my own uncertainties had begun to surface as quite often they did, uncertainties about me, who I was, and certainly, a big question about how and why I was a doctor. And how I got here, taking care of sick "old people without a future," they said, and I figured I had no future either. Was that it? Maybe, but in my mind, Mrs. Segars was boiling up too many shaky questions for which I had no answer, and I felt I was being strangled. I smiled a little, thinking, then telling myself: *But you're a doctor, a physician, a healer of the lame and sick, and master of your own destiny.* Darn! I hated that idea right then.

"What'd you do?" I asked, humbly and caringly, while twirling my thumbs around one another in my lap.

"That's when I returned to New Orleans," she said. "I was a different person...changed from the angry young girl I was when I left. And you know what?" she asked. I shrugged, at the same time thinking a bolt of lightning might fire through the window and strike me because I didn't want to be a doctor. I wanted to be an actor. "Well, my John made sure I'd be well provided for and I really didn't have to work, but all of my life I had done so, and at age thirty-two was definitely not the right time for me to stop. Luckily, I found a wonderful position with the symphony, a place dear to my mother, and to me. And there, I was privileged to rub shoulders with many of the greatest musicians of our time." She looked straight in my face. "Dr. Marquise," she said, "I'm sure you would love to have had a glass of wine with Pavarotti, wouldn't you?" She laughed softly. I came very close to saying, "Frankly, my dear, I don't give a damn!" and would have, but it wouldn't have worked with my blinking the tear from my eye at the same time.

"Yes, I'm sure I would," I said. "I love red wine with Italian food, and Pavarotti's my favorite." A tremor struck me when her face went into disbelief, but I figured again that I was adding to her stories, to her fantasies. And whether they were just a bunch of nothings didn't matter because I could tell they made her happy, and I was glad. Quickly, I asked a question and I knew it had to be a great one.

"And of all the events that made up your life, Mrs. Segers...what would you say was the one event that stands out the most...the one that made you the saddest, caused you the most heartache you ever had. Which one was that?" And too, the doctor in me wanted to get to the crux of her story, her problem, and I was proud of my question when I saw her eyes brighten and her face relax from the disbelief I'd seen a moment before. She raised her hand and pointed a finger at me as her mouth opened, but she stopped, her unblinking eyes set on my face. It was then I knew I should leave, like Rhett left Scarlett, but I wasn't as stupid as Rhett and I loved Celeste.

"Good things and bad things happen during a lifetime," she spoke softly and distinctly, "and I believe we've both had our share. Many years ago I'd recognized that the worst happening resulted in the most marvelous event in my life... what irony, strange, isn't it, Dr. Marquise that you would even ask such a pertinent question." Her voice came louder as she looked straight into my face. "So...I returned to New Orleans over thirty-five years ago, determined I'd rectify, somehow, someday, the worst of the bad events, the one that had tortured me every moment and ate at my soul."

I figured then, she was standing on the edge of a deep chasm, ready to jump, ready to end it all, like so many of my other patients would want to do if they could just think good enough. So I waited. I'd become enthralled in her tale and wondered how she would eventually go, if she would jump, and end it with a lot of yelling and screaming.

I crossed my arms over my chest and stretched out my legs, trying to relax, trying to put my far-reaching thoughts in some kind of order, an order that made sense relative to *my* life. For almost an hour, I had seen an old lady with a story she wanted to tell, but my time with her was now reaching an end, I knew. I wanted her to hurry, speak quickly, because what I was hearing was becoming unimportant, slowly being jumbled, and getting difficult for me to correlate and hold.

"If by the grace of God," Mrs. Segars said then stopped. Her eyes filled with tears, and again she let them roll down her cheeks. "If by the grace of God my mother *had not* died when she did, I doubt that you and I would be here today."

"Oh," I said, wondering what her mother had to do with me. "That's a stretch I don't see, Mrs. Segars. Tell me." My hands were shaking. I sat up straight in the chair and my breaths came faster.

"Like I said, we would be strangers, and I wouldn't be looking this moment into your beautiful green eyes, or seeing your black hair as mine once was," she said, her chin rose as another tear ran freely down her cheek. "I promised the mother who raised you, that I'd not reveal myself as your birth mother until after her death, but now, I'm the one who's leaving soon, and I want you to know about me, and know who you really are." She began to cry.

Celeste's words baffled me, but her sense of commitment was overwhelming, and I never liked being overwhelmed, especially by trivia. I stood quickly, looking down at a woman who I now suspected was just plain goofy. A knock sounded and the door opened. Nurse Sabatini strutted into the room, and behind her was a man in a long white jacket, quite similar to the one I had borrowed from the chair in Sabatini's office. And that rascal had a new stethoscope hanging around his neck.

Nurse Sabatini looked at me, and the creases cutting across her forehead were two inches deep. And like usual, in her puffed-up cigarette voice, she ordered: "Okay, Eddie Boy, head out to the dining room and listen to the singers. You've pestered Mrs. Segers long enough, and put that lab coat back in my office!" she yelled, as I ran.

Just like some of the others, Mrs. Segers screamed when she went over the cliff, and she yelled some of the dirtiest words I'd ever heard.

When I got to the dining room, the piano was dancing like crazy and all the old ladies in wheelchairs were singin' and clappin' while those three women sang about *bringing Jesus on home*. Adrenalin was floodin' all over the place, so I did a jig right there in the dining room door when I heard their words, then shouted, "Amen, amen!" with my fist in the air. I knew right where I could find a brand new stethoscope, and I'd be waiting next Wednesday, when those women would bring a famous man like Jesus to live with us at Sunny Acres.

HOW SCRAPPLE GOT INTO MOMMA'S KITCHEN

It was going to be a good year. I felt it on the first day. It snowed enough to cover the green grass in our yard.

Back then, in my family, Mom worried best, and enjoyed it, I figured. I was sure Dad never worried, because when you told him something or begged for a dime, he always grumbled, "I don't have time to worry about that!" Then there was my grandfather, who lived with us since before I was born. He helped me with my "worry" if Mom or Dad wanted to get onto me for something. I'd run to his room and slide under his bed, then he'd lock his door. He had a saying, too: "I'm too old to worry anymore." But he did worry about one big thing, the war; in fact, until I was old enough to sit in a chair of my own and listen with him, I thought he was in charge of the war from right in front of his big Zenith radio in the living room. I believed he knew everything there was to know about the war, and he was the first person to tell me that 1945 was going to be a good year.

In early February, long before the summer heat came on, my dad agreed to let the mighty US Army use an old country store-building about a half-mile from our house on a sugarcane plantation in the middle of Louisiana. Dad was the plantation manager, and the old store was owned by the company that owned the plantation. As usual, no one bothered to tell me what was going on and when I asked about this great event, all Dad would say was a warning that I should leave them alone, that I'd be interfering in military matters, and consequences could be bad. But he had a warning about anything and everything I'd ever ask about, so as usual, I just let his half-angry words run off me like water on a duck's back. Besides, I wasn't even eleven yet, and I figured—*who cared about me*...just a skinny little kid who didn't know anything and hadn't been more than a hundred miles from where he was born. Getting caught snooping on the army at the old store was the least of my worries, and besides, my teachers thought I was *slick* about observing details in stories we read, and I even prided myself about how to listen to adults talk without their knowing I was listening. So, spying on the US Army just a little ways from my house would be a cinch in my way of thinking. My mind was made up.

On the day they arrived, I shivered in the dreary cold after waiting for nearly an hour in winter-dead honeysuckle under a cedar tree in the fencerow across the gravel road from the old store. The headlights were specs in the distance across an open field, and my heart started pounding, then they rounded the curve and stopped right in front of me. The engines roared again after a soldier opened the gate for three big trucks to turn into the yard. Slowly, they plowed through the tall weeds and small trees to get to the side and back of the building. Soldiers with pistols hanging from their waists, and a couple with rifles in their hands, stood by while several other soldiers unloaded big pieces of strange-looking equipment painted black, other stuff was hidden under brown tarpaulins, and several wooden crates were carried in. From where I hid, I couldn't make out what they were saying, but by the way two of the soldiers stood still and silent with guns in hand while others quickly unloaded the trucks, made me believe without a doubt, this set-up was top secret.

The next day, I rode my bike back to my fencerow hiding place. Except for the grass and bushes left matted by the trucks, there was nothing to tell that the army was hiding out in the old store. After observing for several minutes that no one had entered or left the building, I crossed the road and hid my bike in the tall weeds at the store's front porch. On my tummy, I crawled across the floor like the soldiers did in the news reel on Saturday night at the picture show. The front door was hanging by one hinge, so I slithered under it, and that's when I felt a splinter rip my new wool jacket Mom said Santa had brought for Christmas. Inside the room, I got to my feet and checked out the rip, but it was too dark to see how much damage had been done. I figured Mom could fix it, but right then, I couldn't waste time thinking about a stupid tear in my coat. My best excuse for a lot of tears and scratches was: "The dog did it."

I glanced around, letting my eyes adjust to the dark. The air was thick with dust that hadn't been stirred up in thirty years, maybe longer, at least for the time since the company paid the plantation workers there and sold them food and anything they wanted, "keeping them in debt for the rest of their lives," Mom explained. Through the dusty air and the darkness, voices came from a closed door in the back. I untangled a spider web from across my face.

Slowly and carefully, with one hand, I followed a wooden counter still in place along the wall and stopped when two bright eyes blinked only a few feet in front of me. There was a hiss, then a longer hiss, and I jumped when the eyes shot by me, headed to the door up front. A raccoon, I suspected, and he'd made its home there, and I would have done the same thing if I was a raccoon and needed a place to live. From what I'd read, they're smart little animals but would bite, and would scratch out your eyes if you got too close.

The voices in the back stopped then, and I held my breath. When they started rumbling again, I crept to the door and waited. They went silent a second time, so I leaned with my ear against the door. Chairs scraped the floor, then silence again, and I decided I had to run, to get out of there, but I couldn't run blindly through the dark. Before I could move, the door flew open and a soldier grabbed me and threw me down, pinning me to the floor with my arms back. Another soldier stood with a pistol pointed to my head. He laughed when he saw me, and tried to console me with a few kind words, like, "It's just a stupid little kid in a crazy plaid coat." Then he asked, "You wanna shoot him, Dale, or do you want me to do it?" The other two men went back to working on the big black boxes standing against the wall.

The soldier with red hair and the pistol laughed, then asked, "Lieutenant Rudy, let me pull out his fingernails, would you?" The lieutenant didn't answer, and by then, Lieutenant Rudy was telling me everything was all right. The soldier with the pistol laughed again, but I knew everything wasn't all right at all—I'd been caught and if they didn't take me off to the brig, I knew I would have to suffer the consequences with my dad after they told him they'd caught me spying. Either way, I figured there was trouble ahead.

How Scrapple Got Into Momma's Kitchen

All three soldiers kept working on the equipment with a hundred buttons and dials with faces similar to the face on my grandfather's big radio. They played with wires that ran over the floor from one black box to another, and Lieutenant Rudy made me sit beside him while he asked me a bunch of questions. "So," he said, finally, "you're just checking us out and you belong to the man who runs this farm?" *He's gonna take me to my dad for sure*, I thought, and that's when I recalled how cool the floor always is under my grandfather's bed, but I wanted to tell the lieutenant it wasn't a farm, it was a *plantation.*

"Yes, sir, that's my dad," I mumbled with my head down, hoping the lieutenant would go easy on me if I looked sad and sorry for having caused a ruckus. And if that didn't work, I was prepared to cry and plead for mercy.

"Well, you can come here anytime you want, just come to the back right there, and call to us," the lieutenant said. He patted me on the back, and when I cut my eyes to him, he pointed to the door going to the outside. "Just don't tell anybody we're here."

For the next week or two, every day after school I rode my bike to the old store. First, I'd observe everything outside in the back, strange things I'd never seen, all hidden from the road: the wires coming out the wall, and a big round thing that looked like a bowl, ten feet off the ground connected to the wires. *This is the kind of stuff Buck Rogers plays with,* I thought, and *I'm gonna like it.* And every day when I called out at the door, one of the soldiers would okay my entering their secret place. By then, I'd come to believe that Lieutenant Rudy, by far, was my favorite soldier there, and he was in charge. He gave me food from tin cans, and sometimes a swallow of water from his canteen to wash it down. Then he gave me a canteen of my own, to bring my own water; McHugh gave me several colorful patches like those they wore, and he sewed a couple of the patches on my old windbreaker. I'd become brave by then, called everyone by their name, except Dale. He was the strange one, with black eyes in dark circles, coal-black hair, and he always looked like he needed a shave. He never smiled, and I saw real quick-like, he didn't care for me, because he never talked to me, and never picked on me, so I figured I couldn't trust him and he might get me in trouble with Lieutenant Rudy. One day, I asked McHugh about Dale, but McHugh just grinned and said Dale was okay, but didn't like being in the army, especially way out in the country, hiding in an old building. Then I asked him what was going on with all this stuff, the wires, the black boxes, and that big round thing up off the ground out back. "Nothing," McHugh said, "just listening."

Every day I went to the old store, "headquarters" I called it when I talked to myself about it while sitting at my desk in school. On Saturdays, I'd spend the whole day with my new buddies, and on Sundays after church and dinner in Momma's kitchen, I'd go. And Sunday was the day I'd polish their boots and they paid me a nickel for each pair, and I'd check the duty roster and get another nickel from whoever's turn it was to sweep the floor around the wires. Sometimes they'd let me listen through headphones as big as grapefruits, to squeaking sounds and words they said came all the way from Europe. The names of some of the places they talked about I recognized because before we were allowed to eat supper every evening in Momma's kitchen, my grandfather reported the war news to the family, and never would an evening go by that he didn't mention London, Berlin, Rome, or Moscow, some big city fifty thousand miles from our house. Sometimes he'd tell us that one of our cousins might be pretty close to Berlin or Rome. Like me, my cousins were his grandsons, seven of them in the army, and Momma said if it didn't end soon, I might have to go, too, but I couldn't worry about that, not yet anyway. Then Grandfather would end his little speech with a warning to never touch the dial on his big radio, and that's when he'd look at me, his last glance around the table, and then he'd smile. I figured *I* was his favorite grandson.

After a couple more weeks at the old store, I believed I'd learned more than I needed to know, listening to McHugh and Woodard swapping lies about girls, while Dale grunted every now and then. And dirty words were plentiful when they talked and laughed, but Lieutenant Rudy often told them to shut up and cut out the dirty talk in front of the kid—me. I didn't care one way or the other because I'd heard most of those words anyway, on the playground at school and right there on the plantation, but I'd never put them in sentences except to make McHugh and Woodard laugh. Besides, I knew Mom would kill me if she ever heard me talk that way. And I wanted to tell the lieutenant I didn't believe I was a kid anymore, not with the insignia patches I wore every day and how I could talk just like the other soldiers.

One day in late April, it was hot and clouds started rolling in from the east about the time the school bus dropped

Look Away, Look Away

me off from school. At home, I hurried to close all the windows so Mom wouldn't have to do it. She hadn't believed me back a few weeks when I told her the dog had ripped my new coat, so I figured I still owed her. When I got back to the kitchen, Mom handed me a brown paper sack of homemade cookies she wanted me to take to "those poor soldiers in that horrible old building," the way she always described them. I hopped on my bike, peddling in the wind and every now and then a drop of rain as big as my thumb would splatter on my cheeks. The door was locked, so I knocked and called to let me in. Rain was pelting me while I hugged the bag of cookies and thank goodness, the door flew open just before a strike of lightning hit a tree not far away. Lieutenant Rudy grabbed me, pulled me inside the room, and shook me for a second then fussed, said I shouldn't be out in a storm like that, and why would my mother let me do it. I never said "mother," she was Mom, or Momma. But inside the room, McHugh and Woodard were laughing, dancing, and humming with their headsets on in front of the big black boxes. Dale was listening with his finger on a switch, and he even had a thin-lip smile across his face. Lieutenant Rudy hugged me, then held me by the shoulders and said straight into my face: "Adolph Hitler has killed himself in Berlin."

"You mean, that damn Hitler?" I asked, smiling, ready to join the jubilation. For as long as I could remember, there had been a bad man named Hitler that everyone hated, and I'd never heard my grandfather say "Hitler" without "that damn" in front of that rascal's name.

"Yeah," Lieutenant Rudy laughed, "that damn Hitler, but it's not for us to tell anybody."

How Scrapple Got Into Momma's Kitchen

The next evening after supper, my grandfather told us "that damn Hitler committed suicide, and," he said, "it won't be long now that the war will end." I never told him I already knew it, that I'd learned the news the evening before with the soldiers in the old store.

A week or so later, before Mom cleaned up the kitchen after supper, she handed a brown paper bag to me, this time half-filled with fried chicken, extra she had cooked for those poor soldiers. She gave me another bag with tea cakes and told me to be home before dark set in.

Lieutenant Rudy, McHugh and Woodard, and Dale, too, had been my best friends for a long time, and every chance I got, I'd bring food from Mom's kitchen, homemade biscuits and syrup were plentiful, along with chicken, roast, and pork chops, because we raised most of our food on the plantation. But it was fun to sneak the food out of Mom's kitchen when she wasn't looking or not at home, and I figured, all along she knew about it, just never complained or got on to me because she knew I was taking it to the soldiers.

But that day when I handed Lieutenant Rudy the sack of chicken and cookies, he shook his head, then told McHugh to let me listen on his headphones while they ate a bite. Within three minutes, Dale cut his black eyes toward Lieutenant Rudy and McHugh and motioned for them to listen in, but by the time I handed the headphones to McHugh, I'd already heard. A few minutes later, we started yelling, dancing with each other while only Dale and Lieutenant Rudy listened. After a little while, the Lieutenant raised his hand and we waited to hear what he had to say, but tears had already come to his eyes. He stood and we hugged in one big group, and no one said a word. That's when I knew for sure, that I was a soldier, too.

A big thing had happened that day, and according to Lieutenant Rudy, the entire world was going to change, but I didn't want my exciting world with the soldiers in the old store to change, not now, not ever. I liked it. After so much time with my friends, I'd become their trusted skip-and-fetch it, "the biscuit boy," they called me, and in return, they'd shown me a glimpse of the future with gear and equipment that, until now, only Buck Rogers had used. And they told me about being away from *their* home, *their* families, about being lonesome, about fear, and about war. I was older then, much older than any other kid in my fifth grade class.

The next night at supper, my grandfather stood at the end of the table and said a prayer thanking God for a million things, and I watched with one eye half-open. When he said "amen," I straightened myself in the chair, knowing after a prayer like that Grandfather would have something else to say, something important, and I knew it wasn't a complaint that someone had messed up the dial on his Zenith. What he would say, would make my family happy, and I remembered Lieutenant Rudy had said, "It isn't for us to tell anybody." I smiled. Grandfather was different that night. He glanced around the table first, cleared his throat, then looked down for a second. When he raised his chin, a tear slid down his cheek. "The war in Europe has ended," was all he could say. He sat down to supper, and cried.

A few days later, Lieutenant Rudy's wife arrived on a train from Pennsylvania and stayed at our house, because,

Lieutenant Rudy told me, "your dad's not going to charge any rent." After a couple of days, I'd fallen in love with "Dot" and wanted to marry her. She helped Mom clean the house and Mom did a very rare thing...she let Dot cook supper off and on during the weeks she lived with us. Dot would serve crisp slices of a tasty food, something unique to where she lived in Pennsylvania, and in her direct way of speaking, she'd smile and say: "And don't ask what's in it, young man; just call it 'scrapple.'" Then she'd kiss me on the forehead and scruff-up my hair. And always, Momma made sure Dot cooked enough for the poor soldiers in that horrible old building.

Since 1945, a very good year as it turned out, I've always believed that Lieutenant Rudy, McHugh, Woodard, and Dale rallied for our country, and I rallied, too, when we made a crumbling old building into the finest *listening station* there ever was, but this story is about *scrapple*, and how it got into Momma's kitchen.

SOUL
MATES

I was concerned, shaking like the last leaf on the last tree after a tornado hit. And confused as well. I couldn't figure out where I was, and there was no light on a hill that I could go to, no sounds to lead me into another direction. So, maybe I'd been struck by a bolt of lightning. No, that neither...I couldn't smell burning flesh. *Darn,* I thought, and suddenly a strange feeling of deep loneliness sucked my breath out. I gasped for air, several times, desperate that someone take my hand, hold me in their arms, console me, but I was alone, and in the bit of consciousness that remained, I knew my body was shutting down...gray was all around me, then black took over as my eyes closed. I'd crossed the threshold into another time and place...surely, I had died.

But, the feeling of hopeless gloom was still with me, and I was resolved to accept the situation I was in, but after a few seconds, the desperation I'd felt seemed to abate. I took a deep breath and somehow accepted all of it as part of my *being,* the way I was. *And so it is, forever and ever*, I said softly, and the words shook me. I couldn't figure why such a thought and words had popped into my head. I closed my eyes for a second and was sure I had accepted the idea that that was the only way I could go on this inevitable journey, acceptingly and compliant at each turn I came to, and with no one complaining; so, I knew in a short time, my journey into eternity would soon be out of my control. *I am who I am and there's no changing it.* The how, when, or why were totally disregarded in the format of information that clicked through my mind like an annoying ticker tape impossible to ignore at the bottom of the TV screen. But then, what came next on the ticker shocked me: *You're a dead man now*, it read, so emphatic and mean, but after only seconds, those words didn't bother me at all—important of course—but I reacted with a question to myself: *You stupid bastard, why did you let this happen?* But I had no answer...I didn't know anything at all had "happened." But I thought about heaven then, and knew I wasn't there, had not arrived, at least not yet, and that idea bothered me none at all, because even in the existing quandary, I understood that I'd be in a period of transition, reviewing my life and taking action to finish undone task with people whose lives I had touched. So at the moment, I was suspended someplace between earthliness and eternity, and in my mind, I was confident I'd have a future as long as time itself. That thought, *about time*, shook me badly, however, because in my earthly life, I had been an impatient man, but surprisingly, being confounded by such complicated thoughts vanished quickly, and I was okay about a forever-and-ever existence where ever I might land, and I was sure I could find something to keep myself occupied.

In the dim light, I was surprised to feel myself moving effortless, floating smoothly, and came to a tall, white wall. I glanced right and left and up and down. *Impossible,* I thought, so I turned and leaned with my back against it to see from where I'd come, but there was only a dull, gray darkness, a blank page that I could see. I slid down the wall but a fine, overstuffed chair covered in black silk caught me before I hit the floor. Right in front of me, then, was a purple curtain made of soft velvet. At that moment, music came from far off, sounds of an orchestra playing in the distance. I searched through the folds of velvet but couldn't find an opening. The music became louder as the refrains of the melody surrounded me, relaxing me, and I closed my eyes. A picture surged through my mind...I could see myself sitting in the first chair of the violin section of our local symphony, a position I cherished and envied, and then my mother's voice echoed through my head, that it was her fault for permitting me to quit violin lessons when I was twelve. "Yes, Mother, it is your fault, your fault, your fault." The voice faded away.

I've been dropped in a church; the thought hit me, as the music played on. It was soothing, a marvelous tune I'd heard several times before, *but not about Jesus or God*, and then it came to me...I'm at a wedding? Whose wedding? Darn, I hated having to sit through a wedding, but the feeling at that moment was good, was familiar, and I soon discovered the scene was nearly unchanged from my own wedding almost thirty years before. Happily, like a fairy with wings fluttering, I hovered contentedly, recalling flashes of my happy life.

I blinked and stood, then on the other side of the purple curtain, glaring at a podium covered with a million colorful flowers and a heavily carved rostrum. Behind the rostrum, a rotund man in a long black robe waited. He had no face. When the music finally died, the faceless man moved to the front of the rostrum and stood there. I turned then, and from the shadows, I looked across an assembly of two or three hundred people in the church, and most were like the man in the robe, without a face, only a large, round smear where eyes and a nose should have been. After a couple seconds, I found a familiar full face, one I had known in life...the beautiful face of Elizabeth Warring, so young, so gracious, and surprisingly, she took on the appearance of my college sweetheart. I wanted to cry, but that emotion dissipated quickly. *Beautiful Elizabeth*, I thought. So beautiful she glowed like a diamond glistening in the sun, and stood apart from everyone around her, especially the hundreds of smeared faces. Others, however, I recognized as friends during my earthly life. There was Henry, whom I'd known in high school, still a kid with freckles and pimples, and then Maxine, whom I'd encountered several times during college years. *Poor girl*, I mouthed, as the thought shot through my mind, *she's still a sophomore on the backseat of Rodney's old car.*

With what I had seen in the crowd, I was afraid I'd been dropped into a *time warp*, and then I remembered a familiar saying: "You'll be known as you were known." I rubbed my eyes again with my fingers. "Well, I'll be darned," I said softly, confirming my acceptance of the words I'd heard in Sunday school a long time ago about Heaven.

Again, I glanced to the podium, just as a young man came around the tall, white column and stood next to the man in the black robe, and I recognized readily, my son Jacob. I felt a stir inside me, and deducted then as to why beautiful Elizabeth was in the audience, had traveled over five hundred miles to be there. It was then that I noticed that the flowers covering the podium were all black and white, no color at all, and then I set my eyes on my tuxedoed son and sighed deeply. *Your youngest child's wedding,* came across that annoying ticker tape moving inside my head. I closed my eyes, touched my brow with my fingers, and gently rubbed. I opened my eyes and ten feet away was Jacob's beautiful mother, Helen, my wife, seated in the second row. She cleared her throat, and I was sure it was an attempt to get my attention, so I raised my hand and smiled. Low and behold, there was a man sitting beside her, a young man, me, when I was twenty-five or so, and I was dressed in a tuxedo, relaxed to the point of near embarrassment, obviously asleep. Helen smiled when she glanced at me beside her, and I remembered that before sunrise that morning, we lay in bed anticipating the day, the ceremony, and seeing so many people we'd not seen in a very long time.

With a dark mask of seriousness covering his face, Jacob's eyes searched through the crowd. His eyes...Jacob's eyes are blue, so blue you can see his soul, like mine had been many years before, but mine were dark now and Helen said I gave the blue ones to Jacob. Jacob's eyes had fascinated everyone since the day he was born.

And then, from my spot beside the velvet curtain, I glanced back to Elizabeth and smiled to myself, recalling how fascinated she was of Jacob's blue eyes, wanting to touch them with tiny fingers the first time they played in our backyard. When I saw Jacob glancing about the way he was doing, I knew why when suddenly his smile exploded, then as quickly as it came, it vanished. His eyes then turned bluer and brighter, while his lips moved, silently exclaiming: "Elizabeth."

Something cut through me like a sword, making me wince, and I grabbed the velvet curtain with both hands. A picture of our neighborhood developed in front of me and then a flash of Elizabeth and Jacob as little children, grade school kids, and then high school seniors at a prom. They were clinging to each other and tied by a white satin ribbon. But the bow began unraveling and the ribbon floated away in a breeze. Then Elizabeth and Jacob were swept away, spinning in opposite directions. I felt a tear slide down my cheek, and when I looked, Jacob's eyes turned black.

Just as the flutist finished a special selection of music so woeful I figured Helen would cry, I pulled back the curtain and in the back of the crowd, Elizabeth was searching in her purse then wiped her tears with a tissue. The organ began blaring. In my new situation, outside the earthliness of which I once was, I realized my soul was again in deep conflict with recent human senses. I jerked on the curtain with all my might.

Why was I thrown back here? That question flustered me and the letters of the words floated in front of my face, again as annoying as the TV ticker. *Why back to this...this familiar, crazy event that shouldn't have happened so long ago? Why...but Jacob and Elizabeth are soul mates and they belong to each other.*

I lost control. "Stop, stop," I yelled, my voice I knew didn't belong there, but the words echoed through the church then bounced back toward me, moving the purple curtain as a breeze would do, but no one heard my cries, no one—except one person, Helen. Her eyes moved quickly, searching in the direction of the curtain. "Stop," I yelled again, then jumped up and down, waving, "Stop this thing, it's wrong…all wrong, and I know it…wrong." My voice died away…"Just not right," came out in a whisper. I focused then on Helen. She appeared satisfied with a smile on her face, but I couldn't help but yell at her: "Why don't you stop it, you know we're not soul mates, stop it, stop it, stop it," I yelled, but Helen never moved or spoke a word.

A real sensation came over me, unbelievable, and I felt the blood rush to my head, knowing, even in my new situation, that I should have told my son about love, a spectacular love that lasts through time, through trials and tribulations, through other loves and others' lives, through graduations and weddings, a love that never dies. "It's called first love," I yelled, and again, nobody heard. Then the words from a song I knew a long time ago were crossing the ticker tape, words about "Young Love." I wanted to sing out, right then and there, and I remembered singing it to Jacob a thousand times or more when he was a baby, when I rocked him, because I was a believer; I knew everything there was about first loves, and young love. "But you didn't fail with Jacob," I read aloud as the ticker tape moved on.

I turned quickly and was startled as I glided right through the velvet curtain into pitch darkness; my figuring *black* was symbolic for deeds I'd left undone, responsibilities I'd neglected when I was in full life. In the black around me, dejection hammered my heart, making me want to cry, and when I looked up, there was a piercing white light far away, speeding toward *me*. I raised my hand to shield the glare, and magically, the light vanished, and I burst into the brightness of another day.

There was my own Helen, sitting at the desk in our bedroom, reading at her computer. She laughed softly and took a sip from a cup, then turned and glanced toward the opened door through which I had just glided, fairy-like. She shivered for a split second, my thinking I'd created a breeze, and possibly, she felt my presence. I stood close to her, wanting badly to touch her hand, take in the familiar aroma that always permeated the air around her, an aroma I had come to love. I knew, however, that I could never again touch her hand, her cheek, or sooth her tears, not in my newer state. The thought of my *newer state* somewhat soothed me.

It was tea in her cup, I noticed, and when I glanced up, I decided to read the e-mail on her computer:

Dear darling Helen: As you well know, I was in the crowd at Jacob's wedding yesterday. At this moment, I feel like a high school kid again. And after nearly thirty years, I still believe we are truly the soul mates we always thought we were, and it is our time now and forever. I love you, Mark.

I was angry for a split second that Helen was receiving a love note from a man named "Mark," but upon examination of my memories, I resolved that during our entire married life, Helen had surrounded me with a sense of absolute loyalty. After reading the letter, I sighed and patiently hovered there beside her, sad in having violated her privacy.

But what could I do? In my new state, I had not yet fully received *all* the intricacies of changing an outcome by pointing a finger, or just wishing, but after the hand and light thing a few minutes before, I felt I was gaining the power to affect results by merely being in the presence of the situation. I cherished the idea. There was a lot I wanted to change.

I sat in a chair in front of the bedroom window, watching Helen type away, presumably to her old friend Mark. I glanced to the computer, but was embarrassed to think I was anxious to read what she was writing. *But what the heck?* I squinted and leaned closer, and I was jolted by the few words I was able to catch. *"Like you,"* Helen had written, *"I too have always believed everyone has a soul mate, maybe their first love like you and..."* and darn, the curser was on SEND and she fingered the mouse. And with the leftover feeling from my *old self*, I wanted to tell her I was sorry I'd never felt her pain, never believed that she had longed for her first real love, her soul mate. So...I felt useless, bewildered, then suddenly excited when I felt my earthly perceptions and emotions being washed away, knowing I'd be clean, ready to enter into another time. But outside the window, the trees swayed violently, and I was swept into the wind, above the trees and across the city, racing like a comet through a midnight sky.

A hand tapped my shoulder; I stood straight up pretending I was anticipating the next step in the event. The organ blared a marvelous tune I'd heard before, all in perfect time to watch Elizabeth being escorted down the aisle to where Jacob waited beside a heavily carved rostrum. I looked at Helen as she glanced to the back of the crowd. She smiled.

"Mark," she whispered.

WILLIE

AT WILLIE'S FUNERAL

A mound of dirt lay to the side. Black earth, it's called; old dirt not turned for over a hundred years.

He glanced across the expanse of headstones, crosses, and angels then sat beside me. I smiled and nodded. I wanted to wrap my arms around my brother but in front of all the people there, that gesture would have upset him. I waited for him to say something, but nothing came. I took Donald's hand and moved it to hold in my lap. He sat straight up in his chair, offering nothing, no words, no smile, nor sweet glance. I nestled against him and then looked at his lily-white face and piercing blue eyes. Donald's were bluer than mine, eyes we inherited from the strong-willed Irishman, our father John Abbott, who taught us to laugh and love one another, and to do as he had done—bloody the nose of anyone, in defense of our heritage.

For two days, a slow rain cooled us, but now the skies were deep blue, making for a typical fall day in New Orleans. Pools of rainwater between the graves sparkled like diamonds in the sun; a mournful horn sounded from the Mississippi, and marble angels with broken wings watched as they guarded the homes of the dead. I squeezed Donald's hand and again, glanced at his face. *Unyielding,* I thought, and

I smiled, figuring that even at a time like this, I shouldn't expect him to change from the way he had been all our lives.

I stared at the two red roses on the casket and sighed as the smell of black earth conjured childhood memories of Willie, of springtime, and planting flowers.

The preacher's voice rumbled like thunder rolling in from Lake Pontchartrain, and his words did nothing to ease the pain in my chest from holding back emotions. "Let it go, baby. Let it go," Willie would have said.

How I wished Dad was beside me, too. With thick black hair, always perfectly groomed, he had the handsomeness of a movie star...Clark Gable my friends said. I had heard him described as "charming" and "captivating," but to Donald and me, John Abbott was just the bighearted father who entertained us on the front porch swing with tales about bunny rabbits and dragons, but his best were about our town, New Orleans. And of all his stories and tales, my favorite was about Willie, beautiful, loving Willie. Again, my eyes set on the two red roses.

Like thunder, words rumbled out of the preacher-man. I held tight to Donald's hand; the blue skies faded while the sounds of the city went silent.

THE DREAM

He hugged me, and then laughed...I heard his laugh, Dad's laugh, over the rhythmic squeaking of the front porch swing. I glanced to his face and he smiled, and with his arms around me, I knew I was safe...and I was loved. His words were clear.

"In 1920, New Orleans was already bad, an old city, big and boisterous, a somewhat bawdy show, where liquor was cheap, dancing girls and pimps plied the streets and back alleys of the old French Quarter. And on that enormous stage there was drama, too, about history and traditions that sometimes forgot the *mores of the time,* even those regarding the color of a person's skin.

Wherever you ventured was gilded wealth, but around a corner might be poverty as old as the city itself, and obscure faces of people with no names. Through hot summers and wet winters, old buildings fall away after years of nobody watching, and vines with orange trumpets cover them, hiding history, and hiding the faces in varying shades of color. Other faces follow the vines to another corner where no one watches and no one cares.

But magic takes over where iron balconies shade busy sidewalks, and bright banners wave their excitement in gentle breezes. Visitors mingle with the lively souls who set the stage each day, those who creep from their rooms over the cafes and saloons before the sun comes up, and then iridescence swirls and blends inside this giant kaleidoscope heralding the city as the fun capital of the nation.

Rich with magic and mystery, it's known as New Orleans; romantically, it's called The Crescent City.

SUPPER WITH WILLIE AND GEORGE

Aromas from suppers cooking in the neighborhood of small shotgun houses cast a spell over me as I walked from the trolley on Saint Claude to the steps that led to a narrow porch. I'd made the evening trip from my office downtown to eat supper with George and Willie, my friends who lived in one of my rental houses on Louisa Street, where Willie made sure George and I sat down to the best food in all of New Orleans every evening at suppertime.

"Well suh, Mista Abbott, how'd yo day go?" Willie asked. Her smooth, brown face glowed as usual and she handed me a tall, sweating glass of sweet tea with slivers of chipped ice crowding the rim.

"Fine, Willie, but this heat's about to get to me. Where's George hiding out?" I asked, and then sat at my place at the table. In the middle, a fruit jar held two red roses, making supper in Willie's kitchen a little bit special. I pulled out my handkerchief and wiped the sweat from my neck, relieved that the sweltering day was drawing to a close.

"George gonna be a little late, I reckon, but he'll be here dreckly. You jist relax for a few minutes, Mista Abbott, and in a little while we gonna have the best chicken dinna you ever had."

Willie grinned. All seemed right in her small world within the walls of the little white house on Louisa Street.

I sipped from the glass of cold tea, hoping she hadn't put too much sugar, and sighed approvingly as the just-right coolness slid down my throat.

"Willie, tell me this: How in the world did you get the name 'Willie'? I've wondered about that for as long as I've known you."

Her pleasant expression changed quickly, my question apparently opened an old wound. She cut her eyes to me. "My daddy give me that name, Mista Abbott, because he wanted a boy baby real bad," she said, then turned away from me. "Him and Momma already had two girls."

She sighed deeply as though preparing to launch into a story she wanted badly to tell, a story that apparently weighed heavily in her mind.

Willie sighed again, turned, and looked squarely in my face. "My name's Willa Mae—Willa Mae Williams—can you believe that, Mista Abbott? And I'm never gonna forgive my daddy and momma for all the bad things they did, and I even hate my name because they were the ones who gave it to me." Her eyes were fixed on my face. "But they called me 'Willie.'"

"I like 'Willie,' too," I said, smiling my approval, hoping to lessen the burden of my question. "It's a good name, strong and happy, like you."

I removed my suit coat, draped it over the chair-back, and stole a quick glance at the sweat spots on my shirt.

"I don't ever wanna be called 'Willa Mae,'" she said, and again I recognized pain and bitterness. "In fact, every time I say it, I hate my momma and daddy mo and mo, and I hate to think it, but they weren't very good folks anyway." She looked directly at me, as her words weighed on both of us. "That's the way I feel," she said softly, her eyes filled with wetness. "And I'm sorry about that." She turned back to the stove.

"Well, Willie," I said, breaking in quickly, wanting to change the subject. "I was gonna wait till George got home, but I can wait no longer." I smiled and spoke as though my secret was only for her. "Willie. I've found a girlfriend, and I think she really likes me."

"Oh, Mista Abbott, that's the best news I've heard all week, and I know George sure gonna be glad to hear it." She smiled and her face lit up.

She stopped stirring for a second, tilted her head slightly, and with squinted eyes, asked the inevitable, "How old is this girl, Mista Abbott?"

"She'll be thirty-five in a couple months." I swirled the ice in my glass. "I'm just glad she'd go out with me at all, Willie," I said, confirming the unspoken. On my next birthday, I would turn fifty.

I looked again at the red roses on the table, waiting for Willie to say whatever was on her mind.

"Well, Mista Abbott," she said, her tone serious again, "nobody could be more proud for you than me and George, and you know something?" I glanced up to her face. "Some things sure don't matter none when love steps in, and I betcha that lady's got a lot of love to give. Is she pretty, Mista Abbott?"

"Well, she's rather tall, maybe five six or seven; about your size, Willie. She has blond hair, and the darkest eyes you've ever seen, plus—a beautiful smile." She listened intently, staring into my face. "Her name's Margaret, and she grew up in the Garden District, not far from Audubon Park—an old New Orleans family." I spoke slowly, watching Willie's face. "She's quiet, and the 'stay at home' type woman, but beyond that...well, you'll have to wait to see her in person one day." I drained my glass in two gulps.

"You reckon she's gonna come to my house and visit?"

"Willie, you and George are my friends, and right now I don't plan any change in our "supper for rent arrangement," even if Margaret and I marry someday," I said softly, and at that second, a rose petal dropped onto the table's white cloth. I pulled the roses toward me and sniffed the aroma.

"Now, Mista Abbott, you know you up to where you sure need to start a family before you get too far 'long." She shook her head. "Me and George ain't never gonna have babies; poor George can't make any." Again, Willie sighed deeply, staring at me. I fidgeted with my tie.

She moved to the sink then back to the stove to stir again. Silence was broken when the screened door squeaked open and George London walked in. He glanced toward me, tipped his head, smiled, and called my name while removing his worn, old cap with "French Market Ice" printed over the visor. He hung it on a hook behind the door, and then limped to the kitchen sink. He coughed a couple of times.

"Well, Mista Abbott," he said, turning and looking straight at me, "I sure hope you had a good day today. And how're you, Willie, baby?" She leaned toward him and, dutifully, George kissed her cheek.

"George, Mista Abbott's found him a girl," Willie blurted, "and she's as pretty as she can be, with dark eyes and a big ole smile. I betcha they gonna be married in no time, George, and have some babies real quick." She caught her breath then looked at me for confirmation, and at the same time, signaling her approval.

"Sho 'nough," he exclaimed, smiling. "How old is this girl, Mista Abbott?" He coughed again, clearing his throat.

"I'll tell you 'bout it later, George, baby," Willie said. "Supper's ready. And everything's gonna be fine, and Miz Margaret will come see us as soon as Mista Abbott makes it all okay. That'll be nice, George?" She patted George's cheek, then turned to the stove, picked up a plate and began serving our dinner. My mouth watered and I licked my lips.

George sat at his place, loudly sipping his tea. He glanced to Willie then back to me. "Well, I'm sure proud for you, Mista Abbott," he said as he leaned toward me, his elbows on the table. His eyes squinted, he nodded while whispering, "You gonna sure like havin' a full-time woman."

"Oh, George, hush-up, boy," Willie exclaimed, popping him on his head. "Ya ought not be talkin' that-a-way. They ain't even married yet."

She grinned while giving me a sideways glance, then placed in front of me what was, indeed, the best chicken I'd ever eaten.

I left George and Willie's that evening knowing there were questions in the minds of my friends, wondering how our relationship might change should Margaret accept my proposal.

The neighborhood of small houses, trimmed in shades of several colors, was abuzz with kids playing up and down the sidewalks and in the street itself, watched over by mamas and daddies stirring the air with fans, while laughing with neighbors sitting on the porch next door. Familiar aromas mingled with the damp air wafting in from Lake Pontchartrain.

A gentle breeze through the windows with the methodical sounds of the streetcar rails, lulled me into a near snooze, but I awakened abruptly to the bright lights and traffic of a busy city where hundreds of late shoppers crowded sidewalks along Canal Street.

A few blocks later, we came upon another neighborhood, a tranquil boulevard, lined on both sides by grand homes with tall columns and wide porches; lacy gazebos with tall, pointed roofs stood elegantly, some dressed for a party, and iron gates in brick walls opened to quiet gardens where flowers bloomed. Tall palms waved lazily. Every direction from my streetcar window was familiar and beautiful, solid and strong, and sheltered by ancient oak trees, their limbs draped with silky gray moss. Cool and misty green...my neighborhood.

THE CRISIS

"Hurry, Mista Abbott, please, sir! Hurry!" Willie cried. Quickly I slammed the phone's earpiece into its hook.

"George is sick, Margaret, and Willie wants me to come see about him. Let's ride over to Louisa Street."

"Oh, heavens no, John. They're *your* friends, darling— you go ahead," she said, as she laid her head on the pillow at the end of the divan. I kissed her cheek. Margaret believed she was, in a family way, making both of us happy.

There was urgency and fear in Willie's voice when she called about George. George London was a tall, slim man with dark skin, and deep creases crossed his brow and cheeks. His hands were gnarled from the years of pulling and lifting blocks of ice into the crushers. By Willie's account, George was nearing his forty-fourth year, but he carried the stature and bend of an over-used man well past sixty. Willie blamed the stale, cold air in the icehouses where George had worked since he was thirteen and commented often that George was "coughin'" up his lungs.

When I pulled to the sidewalk at George and Willie's house, several kids ran to my car, and with their fingers, they wrote their initials in the thin layer of dust on the black fenders. They would chatter and laugh, and tiptoe to look over the tops of the doors to see inside. The car had been my wedding present to Margaret, but now, she would have to wait to learn to drive until after our first-born arrived.

The screen door opened and Willie met me at the steps, apologizing: "Mista Abbott, I'm sure sorry we're late with the rent, but the doctor bills for poor George are awful big." Her lips quivered. "I got me a job to take care of a big house and cook for a nice family over on Napoleon Avenue. I'm gonna have the rent by next Friday." She wiped her eyes with the heel of her palm.

"Willie," I said, "I'm not here about the rent. I came to be with George and you."

"But Mista Abbott, I jist want you to know *right now* that I'm a strong woman, and I can do whatever it's gonna take to get your rent," she said, shaking her head, "because poor George ain't gonna make it this time."

For nearly three hours, Willie held George's hand, sometimes talking loudly, other times whispering in his ear. She smiled in her attempt to assure George that he was prepared to make the journey in front of him. George smiled often, and every now and then, a stray tear flooded a crease down his cheek. Truly, there were lessons emerging from Willie's words, and until those moments, I had failed to see who she really was.

THE TURNING POINT

A strong thunderstorm blew in from Lake Pontchartrain and crossed the eastern part of the city, leaving the air clean and fresh. But the skies opened to a bright, blistering sun, prompting the mourners to spread their umbrellas and pull out their fans. Brown and black were dominant colors throughout, and women sported hats in curious shapes, sizes, and colors.

I glanced at Willie beside me, and then to the opening in the ground where George's casket lay. My nose twitched from the smell of black dirt, but I couldn't help that my stare returned to Willie. She was astonishingly beautiful, her face meticulously made and crowned with soft brown hair, and she was the only person dressed in red. She wore a stylish red hat and shiny red shoes, and carried a straw basket whose contents were hidden under a scarf the color of lemons. A red umbrella dangled from her arm. I thought of Margaret and how she'd been too ill to attend George's funeral.

"Willie, where's the preacher?" I asked. "Everybody's gonna be awfully hot if he doesn't get here soon." A drop of sweat tickled down the side of my face.

"Oh, don't worry, Mista Abbott," she whispered, and leaned lightly against me, chuckling softly. "I'm the preacher today, and I'm nearly 'bout ready." After a few seconds, Willie cleared her throat and the mumbling and chattering stopped. She raised her hand, surprising me again when I saw her fingernails painted to match her dress and shoes. Several gold bracelets jangled about her wrist, and I caught a whiff of perfume.

Willie cleared her throat again and hesitated for a moment. Her brown eyes flickered and closed, and then she began.

"Dear Lord in Heaven, we thank you for these skies of blue; blue skies for George, dear Jesus, to make it easy for him to find his way to you." Several *amens* and two *hallelujahs* popped from the crowd, alerting me, and suddenly, something came over me when I felt the passion inside this woman, and the power that came bursting from her.

"We thank you for George, his time with us; he was kind and good to me, and he always stood tall to take care of the things he knew was right." A glimmer of a smile crossed her face, her eyes opened. "And Lord, everybody knows he never looked down on any man. But now, dear Lord...here I am; I'm just Willie, and I'm giving George to you." *Amens* and *hallelujahs* flooded toward us. Willie's eyes closed. I swallowed hard and blinked.

She opened her eyes, and her chin rose. Still, no one made a sound, and all eyes held to Willie's every movement. From atop the straw basket, she removed the yellow scarf, draped it over her shoulder, and from the basket she took out George's dirty old cap. She blew it a kiss and whirled it down onto the casket. Slowly, she reached again into the basket, pulled out a pair of rumpled, dirty overalls, displayed them for the whole world to see, and then flung them into the hole. Gasps could be heard from the mourners as they looked back and forth at each other. Willie smiled while glancing across the crowd, then reached in again, and pulled out George's boots. She raised them as high as her arm would reach, and then dropped them onto the casket, where they bounced with two loud thumps. Willie placed her fist over her heart, and with eyes wide open, she glared into the blue sky.

"Dear Lord," she called out loudly and commandingly, and the slow, damp breeze stopped completely. "Well,

Lord," she said, and I knew without a doubt that God was listening. She smiled faintly and raised her chin. "That's all of George, now, dear Lord; you got every bit of 'im and you can take 'im on home." With her hand raised high and her head bowed, Willie shouted, "Amen, Jesus! Amen!" and the crowd hummed as she dropped the basket into the grave.

Willie popped open her red umbrella, raising it high above her. She glanced across the mourners, smiled for a second, then turned abruptly and strutted to my car for the ride home to Louisa Street.

Cheers exploded, and applause. I watched as the sun caught the tip of the umbrella that never leaned nor swayed. It stood tall, straight and level, like the woman who carried it.

And Willie London was born.

AFTER THREE YEARS TIME

"But Margaret, I understand how *you* want to take care of Donald and keep this big house," I said, "but you're certainly not up to doin' it right now. You need help." Donald was a timid two-year-old with hair as blond as his mother's.

Again, Margaret was in a family way, and would be delivering our second child in a few weeks. Girl's names were plentiful, to honor a mother, an aunt, or cousin in Margaret's family or mine, and we wanted a girl.

"John, darling, I'm going to walk to the market today and pick up a nice chicken," she said. "And tonight we're going to have baked chicken as delicious as any you ever had at Willie's." Margaret stared intently at me. "Yes, I admit my cooking isn't great, and while I'm learning, I can still rear our two children." She sighed. "And like Mother says, John, you shouldn't be so impatient. All I need is time... merely time, that's all."

"Look at this kitchen, Margaret. It's a mess," I said, motioning to the sink full of dirty dishes left from the night before, and Donald's toys scattered over the room.

She cried softly while a cool, morning breeze moved the curtains hanging limp in the kitchen windows. I kissed her cheek and left for my office in the Vieux Carré.

After an afternoon rain shower, smothering heat hung over the city, and when I pushed open the gate into our front yard, a dreadful odor hit me head-on. Hurriedly, I crossed the porch, stepped through the foyer, and moved quickly into the parlor. At the far end, Margaret leaned to one side with Donald on her hip, fanning away an invisible something through the dining room door.

She was crying with tears moving slowly down her pale cheeks as I stood helplessly in front of her. She tightened her hold on Donald and began to sob, then stepped into my outstretched arms.

"What's wrong, Margaret, what's the matter, sweetheart?" I whispered. Breathing was difficult.

"Oh, John, I'm sorry, I'm sorry," she said, crying uncontrollably.

I pushed back from them. "What's wrong? Just tell me, and...and...what's this terrible odor?"

"Oh, John, it's my chicken. It's in the oven and I can't get it out," she sobbed. "Every time I open the door, the... the...odor chokes me, and I almost throw up." She began slowly sinking to the floor with Donald grasping tighter to her. He coughed as he reached up for me to take him.

I helped her stand, while she held her big, round tummy with both hands bracing the underside. Through the dining room, the odor was stronger and became almost unbearable in the hot kitchen. *It's burned to a crisp*, I thought, but there was no smoke in the room. Donald coughed again as I set him on the table near the open window then scrambled for a dishcloth. I opened the oven door slowly then let it quickly slam closed.

"Margaret, what in the world did you do to that chicken?" I asked, while holding the cloth over my nose.

"I don't know, John. I guess it's just a bad chicken," she said, still crying. "It appeared fresh this morning at the market."

"Well something's badly wrong with it—like it's about to explode." I coughed several times. "Margaret, darling, did you clean it, sweetheart?"

"It was already cleaned, John," she said, her tone was angry. "You know I'm not going pluck a chicken here in our kitchen. Besides, I've never cleaned a chicken in my life." I was sure she felt I'd put her on trial about her smelly baked chicken.

"No, Margaret. I mean, did you clean out the inside, remove entrails and all that stuff: the guts, gizzard, and everything else? Did you?" I winced and held it, knowing what her answer would be.

She glanced through the open window, grabbed Donald from his perch on the table, and hurried to the porch.

Standing in the front door, I watched Margaret and Donald swing back and forth, crying softly amid the odor, which

I figured would linger for days in the rooms and halls of our home. I decided then that I must cross the city to Louisa Street.

REVEALATION

When I pulled to the curb in front of Willie's house, I noticed her front door was painted bright red, and I remembered her dress at George's funeral. I knocked and waited, but no one came. I figured she hadn't returned from work, so I sat on the top step and leaned against a post.

As usual, Louisa Street was bustling with kids playing, nosily laughing, and being children, but after more than two years, none was familiar anymore.

"You waitin' for Miz Willie, Mista White Man?" a small girl's voice asked.

"Yes, I am. You know Mrs. Willie?" I asked, and held my hand out to shake hers. Cautiously, and never taking her eyes from mine, she slowly raised her hand.

"Everybody knows Miz Willie, everybody on Louisa Street and all the way to the canal." She nodded, deliberately making the colorful bows in her hair dance. "She's gonna be home in just a little bit, and you can wait right here on her steps; Miz Willie don't care."

Before I could thank her for the okay to wait, she shouted, "There she is; here comes Miz Willie, now." My new little friend skated toward Willie thirty yards away.

"Good to see you, Mr. Abbott. It's been quite a while," Willie said, extending her hand as she came closer. "How're you, and how's Mrs. Margaret and Donald?" Her smile was genuine, her voice firm and sure.

"Margaret," I stammered, "she's...she's suffering a little at the moment, Willie, and Donald's okay, a little fellow much like his mom. And...how...how are you, Willie?"

"Oh, I'm doing as well as any colored woman could do in this old world," she said, smiling. "So, I'm not going to complain one bit." Willie seemed happy and strong, much as she had always been, but she was different, I noticed, with a genteel quality that was quite becoming. Our eyes met for a second. "I work every day, and I love my job, Mr. Abbott, and that's important. I think you know the Duvaliers; they speak well of you; wonderful people who are really good to me," she said, smiling with pride plainly showing.

"Oh, yeah," I said. "The Duvailiers are kind people, fourth generation New Orleanean, I believe."

"Yes, they are," Willie said, smiling. "Would you believe they took me to New York last year at Christmastime and a trip to Chicago last spring? Isn't that something?" she exclaimed, smiling. There was a natural confidence in her words and gestures. "And next year, they're going to Paris for two months to visit relatives, and I'm going, too." Willie's eyes sparkled, as she looked in my face. "Mr. Abbott, I've seen places I never thought Willie London would ever see." The lock clicked when she turned the key.

I stammered again, "Margaret would like to take a trip to Europe one day before I get too old."

The red door swung opened.

"Come on in, Mr. Abbott," she said, as she laid her purse and umbrella on the divan. "I'm wondering what this visit is all about, but before that, tell me about Donald. I bet he's growing like a weed." We moved through the front room into the kitchen. Everything in the house had changed, except the kitchen table, and in its center stood a crystal vase with two red roses.

"Yeah, Willie, Donald's a good boy, with a disposition much like his mother. He sure is, and now we're getting ready for another baby in about six weeks," I said. "Can you believe it? I bet George would get a kick out of that." For a second, her expression wilted, then a faint smile. "I'm sorry, Willie. I'm sure you miss George a lot, and I'm sorry I brought up his name. Forgive me, please."

"Oh, Mr. Abbott, that's okay," she said, her hand waving the thought away. "Everybody thinks the same as you about George, and he *was* a good man; good to me and to everybody else." Her smile was frozen. "We buried him three years ago yesterday, you know, and right now, memories are difficult, good ones and bad ones." Her smile vanished then. "And nobody knows the entire story, but it doesn't really matter anymore, except to me, I suppose." She patted my arm as if to console me. "Y'all want a girl this time, I bet?" she said hastily. "Mrs. Margaret needs a girl to even things out." Tears glistened in her eyes.

"Yes, we do want a girl," I said. "But Willie, what do you mean by the 'entire story?' What are you talking about?" It was she who needed consoling.

Her dark eyes, under meticulously groomed brows, turned up to mine. "Well, it's a long story, Mr. Abbott... something you don't know about me, and one I've never told anyone," she said, speaking slowly, while motioning me to sit in the place at the table where I had always sat. "I've been waiting a long time to tell the right person; really, I've wanted to tell someone so I can forgive, get it off my heart, and out of my mind." She smiled. "And you know what, Mr. Abbott?" She hesitated for a second. "I've always believed *you* were *that* person, but the time was never right, and then one day...here you are, just when I needed you." Her smile returned. "So you see...I'm *happy* you came to see me today."

Willie brushed a small handkerchief across her forehead, her lips parted, and she sighed deeply. "Did you come to hear my story, Mr. Abbott?" she asked, and then laughed quietly, looking wistfully at me.

"Sure. That's exactly why I came, Willie, and I have big shoulders, and I like good stories," I said teasingly, "big shoulders." Our eyes met again.

"You know, Mr. Abbott," she said, shaking her head and again smiling pensively, "there aren't many white folks who can put themselves in *a colored man's place,* and far fewer who can imagine the life of a colored woman, all alone in *this* old world."

I nodded, and suddenly I felt uneasy, troubled by the idea and the possibility in Willie's statement. I glanced to the floor.

"When I was born," she began, "my momma birthed me one morning in the dew, on the edge of a cotton field about a hundred miles north. She birthed me on two sacks of cotton she and my daddy had just picked. Momma and Daddy were so poor, the next morning they went right out to the cotton field again, picking cotton with me tied to the bottom of momma's sack. They had waited for years, believing they would get forty acres of land and a mule, but that never happened, and they stayed chained to the plantation, just like their parents, and their grandparents. Me, my little brother, and two older sisters were born there, grew up there, and worked alongside them in the cotton, the sugar cane, or whatever job we were given."

Tears welled in Willie's eyes, moved down her cheeks, and fell onto her dress. She brushed the spots with a finger.

"On rainy days or in winter when there was no work in the fields, we would go to school in town, and had to walk almost two miles to get there. All of us loved school and went as often as possible, but one day my two older sisters disappeared, just left, ran away, Momma said, and we never talked about them anymore. Oh, every now and then, Momma would cry a little, but she always got on to something else anytime their names came up."

I was sorry I had never asked Willie about her childhood, about her family, or her background.

"Then one day, in the middle of May, it was too wet in the fields to chop cotton, so Daddy let me go to school. When I came home, there was a man sitting with Momma and Daddy on the porch." Willie paused, staring directly at my face. "He was a great deal darker than me, tall and slim, and he even talked differently than the way we did. I thought that was funny, the way he said certain words, but after a few minutes, I went in the house and Momma followed me and told me to come back out to meet the man. She said he was gonna take me off the plantation so I could go to school and study to be a nurse. That's what I always wanted to be, a nurse to take care of babies. That's what Momma and I talked about, both of us being nurses, but

Willie

poor Momma couldn't even sign her name. Right then, Mr. Abbott, I was almost finished the seventh grade."

Willie stood and offered me some water, then filled two glasses.

"You sure you want to hear all this, Mr. Abbott?" Her smile was slight.

"I do. I sure do, Willie. Every bit of it." I took a sip of water, slumped back in my chair and watched her face and gestures.

"Well, after dark came, Momma and I put my clothes in a pillowcase for me to take. She told me I was going far off, but she didn't know where; the man would tell me when we made it to town. Mr. Abbott, all I could think about was leaving my momma, my daddy, and brother, and thinking 'bout school seemed to help, made leaving easier." Willie glanced to the floor, then back to me. "When we got to the depot in town and saw that big train, I was scared, and I started crying. The man hugged me and told me everything was gonna be okay, and we'd be to New Orleans in a little while. That really made me cry, because I knew New Orleans was a long way from home, and my momma and daddy weren't ever gonna come that far from the plantation to see me. But the man held my hand, and we got on the train. There were a few white folks up front, so we went to the back of the car and sat by ourselves. After a little while, a big puff of steam passed my window, and the racket got awful, but we were on our way to New Orleans. I dried my eyes on the pillowcase. The man hugged me again, then pulled me close to him and placed his hand on my cheek with my head on his chest. He was kind and gentle, while I cried some more."

Willie stopped, eyes brimming, and looked straight into my face. "He spoke softly, Mr. Abbott, and held my head tight against him. 'Willie, baby,' he whispered in my ear, 'my name's George, George London.'"

Again, I wanted to console her, imagining the fear in the scared little girl on the train.

"That's not all, Mr. Abbott. You gonna let me tell you the rest?"

"Absolutely. I want to hear all of it, Willie."

"Well, George and I never married," she said, "because I was barely thirteen years old when he brought me here. George…he was over thirty-seven and worked at French Market Ice for a long time in a steady job. And he told me I could go to school if I wanted to, but being in a big city made me afraid, and made me think differently. George said it was best anyway that I didn't leave the house, and wanted me to be home when he came in from work."

Willie gazed out the window for several moments, seemingly to collect her thoughts.

"Time passed, Mr. Abbott," she said, her lips quivering, "it passed slowly at first, then quickly, and awhile before George died, I figured what happened to my two sisters when they disappeared is the same as what happened to me. And I heard my brother ran away when he was about twelve. He was only nine when I left the plantation. And now, all I've got is myself; and all I know about the years with George *is*…I took his name, that's all he left me, and that's all I have…his name." Willie sighed deeply while drying her eyes. "Momma and Daddy both died a long time back, but I never saw them after I left." Again, Willie stopped and looked questioningly at me.

"Go on, Willie, I want to hear that, too," I urged.

"Well, a couple months before George died, a man came here to see him, and they sat on the front porch talking like old friends. I could hear the mumbling, and I heard the man say my daddy's name, Johnny, so I sat at the window and listened. He told George that my daddy owned fifty acres of cotton land, and when Daddy died, he left it to him. After the man left, George stayed on the porch, so I went out and sat beside him and asked about the man. He acted like he didn't want to talk about it, but I insisted, and he told me that was my daddy's brother, and he lived right here in New Orleans. I never knew anything about Daddy having a brother, and George said he was the one who made the arrangements for me to come to New Orleans." Willie stopped and looked at me with a slight smile, as though her words didn't want to come out.

"And what happened then, Willie?" I asked.

"Mr. Abbott," she said, her words barely a whisper as she cried softly, "for a long time...for a *very* long time...I knew something was wrong with me, wrong about my life from the day I left my family. I felt as though I'd been locked in a box with no air to breathe, and my soul was badly broken, the pieces were scattered. I didn't know who I was, or why I was here, and...I *had* no past; nothing for me to stand on or hold to, and I had nobody...there was nobody to help me find it. But on the front porch that day, the air suddenly cleared, and I caught my breath when the truth came out."

"The truth, Willie?" I stammered. "The truth?"

"The truth, and the facts," Willie said, shaking her head. "Poor George was holding my hand when I started crying, but he wouldn't look at me. He put his hand on the side of my face and pulled me against him, just like that first night on the train. 'Willie, baby,' he whispered, 'I gave 'um two hundred dollars for you, two hundred dollars.' And he started crying, too."

Her stare passed me as she looked into the darkness of her bedroom. Surprisingly, Willie's tears had dried, and she sat tall in her chair. "Mr. Abbott, I was thirteen years old when my folks sold me to a man three times my age."

Her lips quivered, then she smiled, wistful and short. Tears came in *my* eyes as I brushed my fingers lightly over her cheek. With the handkerchief, she blotted away my tears while the scent of her body consumed me. She took my hand and stood.

"Don't cry for me, John Abbott. For a long time now, Willie London's been free."

CHANGES

Within a few short weeks after my visit to Louisa Street, Willie had been woven into the fabric of the daily lives of the three Abbotts on Saint Charles Avenue. She ran the household and attended to Margaret, who was ten days past due for the birth of our second child. Late into the evening of the fifteenth day, Margaret's suffering ended, and life as we knew it came to a halt. She died in our bed and never knew her second child was a girl, and I chose to name her Margaret, to honor her mother.

Though devastated by the tragedy, we moved quickly through a shifting time in our lives, and it wasn't long before we became as happy as we would ever be.

For several years, Willie had taken over the jobs of collecting the rents and handling the needs of maintaining the rental houses throughout the neighborhoods off Saint Claude and Louisa Street. She was the chauffeur, the banker, and confidant for all of us, living in the grand house on Saint Charles, and venturing to the little white house when necessary.

Often, the children walked with Willie to collect the rents, and as she knocked on a door, she always spoke out, "It's Willie London, again. Time to pay the rent," and when the door opened, she'd smile and say, "It sure comes quick, don't it, baby?" The same words at every door, and never would there be a complaint or challenge.

She taught the kids to skate on the sidewalks and play ball in the street. They were at home on Louisa Street and at home in the big house across town on St. Charles.

BACK AT WILLIE'S FUNERAL

My eyes flew open when my body jerked, startled by the powerful voice of the preacher when he shouted, "Amen!" We stood, and I glanced at Donald's expressionless, pale face and pulled my hand from his. Still, he said nothing. I shaded my eyes from the setting sun while watching my brother walk to his car for his ride home to St. Charles Avenue.

"Willie London," a voice said softly behind me.

I turned and smiled.

Like my mother, they call me "Willie."

CHRISTMAS CAKES

"Hurry, hurry, hurry!" she'd say as she quickly moved the dishes from the table, "or I'm gonna miss it." Every evening we gulped our supper so Momma could listen to the news in the living room with my grandfather, who constantly jiggled the tuning knob to cut out the static on his Zenith. Dad didn't bother to hurry because, he said, "it's a waste of time listening to static and not know where they are anyway." "Where they are," was about my seven cousins and two uncles in the army in 1942, fighting somewhere in an angry world.

"That's where they are," Grandfather would mumble when the words "New Guinea" came through the static, and then he'd cup his ear and lean toward the radio in an attempt to hear better. He believed that two of my cousins were fighting there. The other five cousins and Momma's two brothers were someplace else, and no one in the family knew where.

School that year closed for the Christmas holidays on my eighth birthday, a week before Christmas, and wouldn't start again for almost four weeks to save coal that heated our school and gasoline that ran the buses. Four weeks for Christmas was all right with me.

On Saturday morning, Dad shook me to wake up. "Coffee's ready," he said, and by the time I reached the kitchen, he'd put a broken-up biscuit left over from supper the evening before, poured in a little cream, and a heaping spoon of sugar in my cup of coffee. That would be my breakfast. To keep warm, I stood close to the big iron stove, ate the coffee and biscuit quickly while Momma sipped her coffee. After a little while, we cranked up Dad's old truck and left on the start of a Christmas tradition, the first stop being at Dad's sister's store, and then to his brother's house about five miles farther down the road.

The fumes of burned gasoline seeped from the floorboard of the truck. I took a deep breath and rubbed my nose, putting my hand over my mouth as I chewed the corner I'd bitten off of one of Momma's cakes. The misty rain came faster than the wiper could wipe, and with his handkerchief, Dad cleaned the breath fog from the glass in front of him just as I swallowed the last bite of fruitcake. I glanced to his face and was sure he hadn't noticed anything. My Mackinaw, and with my leather aviator's cap securely snapped under my chin helped to keep me warm in the old truck with no heater. I glanced at the brown paper bag beside me, smiled, and licked my lips, knowing that one of Momma's famous fruitcakes wrapped in a soft cotton cloth soaked in whiskey was missing a corner and doubted my aunt would notice. I felt safe.

Our mission was to deliver Momma's cakes, one for Aunt Sook at her store, and another for Uncle Ray and Aunt Inez, who would give us my favorite of all Christmas cakes, one of her famous yellow layer cake dressed heavily with egg-white icing sprinkled with coconut and six red cherries expertly placed on top.

Christmas Cakes

I shoved my hands in my jacket pockets and glanced at Dad just as a puff of blue smoke billowed in front of him. He placed his cigar-holding hand atop the steering wheel. He was a powerful man in my eyes and I was happy to be riding alongside him, "riding shotgun" was the way he put it when he woke me that morning, and I felt "big." On both sides of the road, stretching all the way to the woods, were empty fields, brown and wet, windswept and cold. *But this is Christmas*, I said to myself and smiled for the good feeling. School would be out for a long time, and the best events for the next few weeks would take place in front of a fireplace, our fireplace or somebody else's, where I'd sit cross-legged on the floor, watching the flames, feeling the warmth, and listening to the grownups talk about crops just harvested and plans for spring, or talk about the war, or church on Sunday. But the stories I liked best were about my soldier cousins and uncles, where they might be fighting, hoping they were safe, and wondering when they might come home. Sometimes there were tears around the fireplace, but hidden from little kids like me.

Cold air seeped around the window glass as the old truck hummed. I thought about Momma and her advice before we left home that morning. "Wear your Mackinaw," she'd ordered. "It's Christmas and winter's here. I think it's going to sleet." Sleet was a good word, one I liked every winter, because we all believed it had to sleet before it could snow. And when she said "sleet" early that morning, excitement set in and with it was an abundance of hope, even though I knew that snow seldom came where we lived.

My dad and his brother were farmers who grew cotton on land they didn't own, living in old houses still standing in stateliness, the old homes of wealthy landowners who built them before the Civil War. And as farmers during the fearful war years we were in, we never suffered from the lack of food, even foods that were in short supply at my aunt's store, foods rationed by the government so to feed our soldiers in New Guinea and everywhere else in the world. And one of my jobs for the war effort was to save toothpaste tubes for the lead in them, and gum wrappers for the tin foil, and then make sure they got to the store where I'd drop those little balled-up pieces into glass containers for somebody to pick up later. I was patriotic, Aunt Sook said...and that made me proud.

The brakes squeaked when Dad stopped the truck in front of Harper's Grocery at the crossroads at Morrison's Station. Harper's was the most lovable country store along the ten-mile stretch from where we lived all the way down the gravel highway to the village of Gold Dust, our final destination that morning. Harper's was Aunt Sook's store, and Momma gave a whole fruitcake to Aunt Sook, because "she doesn't cook," Momma said, but mostly as a small "thank you" for extending credit all year till the crops came in and we had a little money.

Dad cut off the switch, and the truck jerked as the engine died. I reached into the brown bag and took out the cake on top, making sure Aunt Sook got the one with all four corners because Momma went to Aunt Sook's store every two days or so, and I knew Aunt Sook would mention to Momma if her cake was missing a piece. As I stepped from the truck, I brought the wrapped cake to my face, and it was ripe and ready—I had proof from the other cake; ripe with sweetness flavored with whiskey. Many years later, I came to realize there was too much dignity and pride in our family to tolerate the idiocy created by indulgence in strong drink...except in fruitcakes Momma made every fall for Christmas. Besides, we were Baptist.

Inside the store, Dad took out his wallet and paid our yearlong grocery bill, and then I handed Aunt Sook the fruitcake. Carefully, she removed the cloth right there at the counter, took in a deep breath of the aroma, smiled, and then hugged me. The first of the Christmas rituals for that year were accomplished.

Sleet bounced off the windshield before the wiper could catch it. Dad looked at me with a smile that I took to mean that snow was coming; it was going to happen. At the front of the big house, he turned the key in the switch and again, the truck lurched forward. I grabbed the brown paper bag, jumped out of the truck, and together we ran through the sleet to Uncle Ray and Aunt Inez's long front porch. After a couple of seconds, the door opened and a colored woman I knew as Rebecca smiled and said good morning. The big foyer was as cold as the outside. We crossed the dark wooden floor to the door to the left, straight into the living room, warmed by a small fire in the fireplace, then into another room as cold as the foyer—the dining room. On the far side of the dining room, Rebecca opened the door into the kitchen, where a fire with tall red flames was roaring in the fireplace. I pulled off my aviator's cap and stuffed it in my pocket, knowing there would soon be a "fireplace" chat. Aunt Inez smiled and told Dad that Uncle Ray was tending the animals at the barn and would be coming in soon. I handed her the paper bag.

"I know what this is," she said, smiling, "and I'm gonna put it in the dining room with the others." The door onto the back porch opened and Uncle Ray walked in wearing his usual khaki shirt and pants, and red-toed socks with no shoes.

"Boy, what are you doin' out on a day like this?" he asked me, smiling, and nodded to Dad.

"Trading Christmas cakes, I guess," I told him, and smiled.

He pulled a straight chair to the fireplace and began putting on his shoes while talking to Dad, mostly then a chitchat about the weather, the sleet, and the possibility of snow. A young colored man entered from the porch. His name I remembered was "Sonny" and was Rebecca's younger brother.

Rebecca and Aunt Inez cooked breakfast and for almost two hours, we sat around the kitchen table, ate, and I listened while the two brothers talked. From other conversations, I'd learned that Mom and Dad affectionately called each other "Pete" and that day, I learned that Aunt Inez and Uncle Ray called each other "Snooks."

A few minutes later, Sonny brought in an armload of wood for the fireplace and it was time for Dad and me to go.

In the dining room, Aunt Inez handed a box to me. "Now be careful, and don't tilt it or drop it. It's your momma's Christmas cake," she said. My eyes were turned up to her kind face. "Be sure to tell her I just couldn't wait so I broke off a corner, and this year's is the best ever." Smiling, she winked at me then brushed my cheek with her fingers.

Like all the other years and Christmases I'd known, it didn't snow in 1942. But while the war raged around a changing world, we were anxious and listened to the Zenith every evening, and we did what we'd always done to keep our lives ordinary, because that's the way we were.

And we traded Christmas cakes.

THE
LAST TIME
I SAW PARIS

We went to Paris a few years back. When we got to the airport in Atlanta, I became lost as a snake in high weeds. It was crazy, and what a mess it was when all we wanted was to find our way to the plane goin' to Italy, which, by the way, was going to be our first stop, not Paris. They ought to not make airports so big, like the one in Atlanta, but the ticket man was kind enough to let a Mexican lady named Miz Rita something or other to lead us to the plane. I have to say, from the way she sounded and all, it seemed to me like Miz Rita was a first-class addition to our society, considering all the rigmarole we hear in the news now days about people comin' up from Mexico. And Miz Rita got us there, and the plane took off headed to guess where…Greenland, according to the TV screen in the airplane. I finally figured out it is shorter to cross over the world that way, rather than try flying around the shape of the Earth itself. Anyway, we headed to Greenland to get to Italy, to get to Paris, and I thought that was funny, not "ha ha" funny, just odd, sort of. A few hours later when everything was dark except for a few people trying to read, around ten, I think, I told a fancy lady next to me that the plane was awfully stuffy from so many people breathing the same air over and over, and all I wanted was to make conversation with the poor old gal, just somebody to talk to. At first she didn't want to talk, but I kept asking her questions and she'd answer with another question, sort of like a stupid game she wanted to play. Finally, she asked me where I was from and when I told her Alabama, she just looked straight at me for at least three or four seconds, then shook her head. I figured then if I'd said New York or Minnesota she would have talked to me, but I figured she didn't know much about "Alabama" and didn't want to look stupid. So she just closed her eyes pretending to be asleep. She was nice and all, but my wife said to shut up and leave the woman be.

Would you believe we got to Rome, Italy, around seven in the morning and got a taxi to take us to the hotel to rest up—seven in the darn morning, to rest up, when I'd been resting-up for over eight hours already and my ankles looked like fence posts. Anyway, that old taxi driver nearly killed us, the way he drove, fast and darting like a deer, in and out of all those little cars with loud horns that never stopped. I figured he was showing off because we were Americans, but anyway, my wife kept squirming and closing her eyes every time we came close to hitting another car, and I finally figured the rascal knew what he was doing; in fact, it was kind of fun doing all those stupid things in a Mercedes Benz—that old rattle-trap was probably twenty years old but still able to go like crazy. After that stupid ride, we rested up at the hotel then took a train to Florence the next morning. That name made me want to laugh. That was my momma's name—Florence. I never said anything about the irony, because my wife and daughter knew my momma and what her name was. Heck, Momma died a couple or so years after we made that trip to Europe; eighty-nine, she was, and

I thought she was old, but believe me, not nearly as old as that old city. In fact, everything there was more than old, even the air looked old; I guess being stirred up with a million or two little cars never stopping. What a mess that was. But we looked at a couple old churches that must have cost a million dollars to build a thousand years ago, then rented one of those little cars the next day to go to Cortona, a little old town on a hill about forty miles south of Momma's town. Now, let me tell you right now, don't do that, rent a car and expect to enjoy driving in Italy, right in the middle of a bunch of crazies.

We finally got on the Estrada, like our interstates, big highways where the cars move fast, and here we were, in a car about the size of our back-door closet. Man, would you believe we got off a couple of times because all the signs were in Italian and we were scared to death in that little old car, but every time we got off, we had to pay to get back on the thing—something like ten thousand lira, or whatever they call their money, but not dollars. Anyway, after two or three close calls from big trucks and a couple of Volkswagens, we finally came to a sign that said Cortona, and all I could do was giggle, I was so glad. By then I was as touchy as a dog in heat from driving that little old car all the way from Florence, and it barely had enough power to climb up the hill to Cortona, to our hotel. We've talked about that hotel several times since then, because that's where they put us on the fourth floor, but the fourth floor was down, not up, down on the side of a hill, and when I opened the door onto the balcony off our room, I could see for forty miles at all the little towns sitting on top of hills, and a big lake way off in the distance. Heck, I thought that was about as pretty as anything I'd ever seen in magazines or books, but I still wanted to vomit for some reason. Anyway, I took a shower and put on some short britches and went up to the lobby. What the devil—none of those people spoke English, so I gave up on a cup of coffee, just went out to the overlook and sat on the bench under a funny-looking tree that was too little to make any shade. Luckily, I'd bought an expandable fan in Florence, a pretty little thing, hand painted with a Flamenco Dancer, a good-looking woman on it, but still, it wasn't the fan I'd picked out if I'd had a better choice. No matter. But then, it wasn't long that two women dressed up in silky dresses and high-heel shoes came and sat by me. They asked me something and I just raised my hands and said, "American." They giggled for a second and looked at each other. About that time, the wind blew up one of their dresses and that woman laughed out loud for a second, making like she was embarrassed or something, but I'd already seen her garter belt way up to her thighs. I smiled and glanced at her while she fixed her dress down. She just smiled back and patted my leg, making me jump a little when she touched me, but I figured she was telling me she was sorry she'd embarrassed me that a way, and not to worry. You can bet I wasn't worried about anything right then, except it was so confounded hot, you know what I mean, sitting in the sun because that miserable tree was so little and my fan just didn't move a lot of air. I'd started sweating, then the woman who had the dress problem reached and took my fan and spread it open, then hid her face behind it for a second or two. I thought she was the prettier of the two girls, and I smiled at her. She folded it back and smiled when she handed it back to me. She clicked her tongue a couple times, you know—like telling a horse to gitty-up, and it was just about at that second we heard the music coming from around the building on the corner. Anyway, I figured it was time for me to move on from that hot spot and just when I stood up, six black men turned the corner from behind the building, headed straight to me, playing "When the Saints go Marching In" and dancing like crazy. I smiled at one of those ladies and walked over to meet those fellows I knew came from New Orleans, Louisiana. Can you believe that? And I was born and raised just a hundred miles from there, almost my hometown. I use to love New Orleans, and went there every chance I got. Momma use to fuss about it, but she got over it eventually, I guess. Did you know, by the way, that a young fellow could go to that old city and do just about anything he wanted and nobody would rat on him later? I got living proof of that, boy. But anyway...

The next morning I met the biggest man in that band, the tuba player, and bought his breakfast right there in the hotel, just him and me. Son of a gun was he ever a big guy, big around and tall, and he told me Cortona was the last stop on their tour through Europe..."eleven months," he said. Well, I figured I was about like him after two days. I was ready to head back to Alabama already, and we hadn't even got to Paris yet.

After I paid for his breakfast, though, he gave me a pass to the concert that night in the piazza, for a spot right in front of the band, for all of us. That was nice, even though we didn't even say our names. But that night was something else. I bet there were five thousand people in the piazza, and we were just standing there by a smart-alecky-looking girl with almost no clothes on. She had chewed-down nails, but it looked to me like she had fresh polish on them—black, and I do believe she had a new set of headlights. I say that because of the way they stuck out and the way she bounced them while the band played. But anyway, she also had a big old dog on a leash, and before I knew it, that rascal peed on my leg. I stomped my foot trying to get rid of the pee, and an old woman in back of me with an ugly little poodle in her arms started laughing, then said something to that darned ugly girl about her big dog, which had a lot of fur and kept trying to smell me. Then all of a sudden, they started fussing about their dogs, that's what I figured, one big dog and one little dog, and I tried to explain that it wouldn't take long for them to get to be friends as soon as they sniffed each other a couple times. Son of a gun, they both got on me for meddling I figured, but anyway, that's what my wife said, and then that old lady—and she had a terrific nose, big and sort of blue—well, she motioned for a policeman standing on the steps about thirty feet away. I told my wife I was leaving, and I did. I went to the other side of the piazza and waited for the choir to start. They were from Chicago, the sign said. I didn't like that gospel kind of singing, so I just wandered around in that darn crowd until almost ten o'clock, then went back to the hotel. I was ready to leave that place, darn it, was tired, come halfway around the world to listen to a band from New Orleans and a stupid-ass choir from Chicago. Darn! I knew I'd be ostracized for the way I thought, so I went on to sleep. I wanted to say good-bye to my friend, that old tuba player, and buy his breakfast again, but when he came up to the lobby the next morning, he said he had the grippe and couldn't eat any breakfast. I sure didn't want the grippe, so I let him be, and I was already pouting with a little bit of anger because I had to take a cold shower. Can you believe that crummy hotel ran out of hot water? Man alive...can you believe that? Well, let me tell you something: every now and then, I appreciate the chance to get a little indignant about crazy stuff, and a cold shower is one of those times. But anyway...

Everybody I know of loves Cortona. That old town is so old you can almost hear the chariot wheels grinding in a race like Charlton Heston did in *Ben Hur*, making the dust rise, and when you look far out, you're looking through pink. But we had to go, so we left Cortona on Tuesday and drove that little old car back to Florence. And boy, believe me, the Estrada was popping, and by the time we got to downtown to catch the train to Paris, my heartbeat was up to at least a hundred and thirty. I could hear it pounding. I was even out of breath by then, but I have no wind anyway, if you want to know the truth. I guess because I used to be a smoker, but they made me cut it out; my kids did. And I'm glad about that, really, but then I started getting a little paunchy belly and can't get rid of that rascal. Isn't that awful?

But anyway, I dropped my wife and daughter off at the train station and I was going to turn in that stupid little old car, but I couldn't find the office. I ended up in the middle of that city with ten million other little cars and a bunch of men and women riding motor bikes between the cars. Would you believe me if I told you that out of all those people, not a one could answer my question about where that darn car rental office was? And the third time around was when I came real close to losing my life, and that's the gospel truth. This is what happened, really, if you can believe it. About twenty yards in front of me, I spied a policeman's helmet over the top of another little old car he had stopped, so I pulled over, and the brakes squealed like crazy. Just when my little old car came to a halt, that policeman raised a tommy gun and pointed it straight at me, about fifteen feet away. Boy did my hands shoot up, and I yelled right away that I was an American. That cop motioned with his thumb for me to move on and when I let out on the clutch, the darn engine died, dead as a doornail, and he started yelling and swung that gun straight back *at me*. Man alive, I turned the key and that miserable little car jumped like a rabbit and took off before the policeman pulled the trigger. Now, I was really grateful for that, and even said so right then, to God. I said out loud, "Thank you, Lord, thank you!" A few minutes later, I found the rental office and had to pay an extra day because the turn-in time was noon and I'd fooled around till almost a quarter past twelve. That was a hell of a note, but what could I do?

Like I said before, I don't have much wind, and by the time I huffed my way back to the train station, I was played out. My wife didn't notice, I don't think she did anyway, but by the look on her face and my daughter's face, I was sure if they didn't get on that train to Paris I was going to be ground meat in five minutes. Believe me, all I wanted to was to get on that train, too, so I never told them about that crazy policeman who nearly killed me right there in that stupid little old car. Even today, when I think about it, I figure I could be buried right now in a pauper's grave in Florence, Italy, and nobody would know where I am. That might sound goofy, but it could happen—you know what I'm saying?

On the train, after running my legs off, I opened the door to the compartment and my wife nearly ran over me to get to one of the long seats, and my daughter knocked my flamenco dancer fan out of my pocket to get the other seat. Heck, I knew what they thought; they'd lie down and take a nap, but where was I going to sit? Anyway, I sat on the seat next to my wife, because I knew she'd let me lean on her and if I asked just right, she'd massage my hands. Boy did that feel good, for her to massage my hands. Has anyone ever massaged your hands? In your life?

According to that darn schedule the travel agent back home gave us, we'd arrive in Zurich around midnight, and when we did, boy was I surprised at that train station; just a little old dinky place and nobody there, not like the one in Florence or Rome. I had to knock on the counter to get some attention, and that's when a sort of heavy-set woman with all kinds of makeup came toward us, primping her hair back in place, and before I could say hello or anything, a man in the back room where the woman had come out of sneezed. All I did was smile at her, then I asked her to call us a cab, and after about twenty minutes, a taxi squealed to a stop at the curb where we were shivering in that cold mountain air. I couldn't believe it was cold, and I had on short britches and my fan was in my shirt pocket like I might need the son of a gun up there in the Alps. The street was shiny wet without

Look Away, Look Away

a soul in sight, not even a moon, but would you believe—I bet there were a million stars I could see. About then, a dog barked way off, and I thought about some crazy bats flying around and about Frankenstein. Now those are good movies, at least *I* think they are. Anyway...Real quick-like, the cabbie loaded our suitcases in the trunk while we warmed up inside the taxi. Mr. Taxi Driver plopped down on the seat, and I told him the name of the hotel and in the dim light, I saw the look on that man's face and knew he wanted to fight. But luckily, all he did was hop out, open that trunk, and throw our suitcases onto the sidewalk. He stood there and looked like he was about ready to pull out a gun and kill all three of us, then he pointed to the red neon sign about fifty yards up the shiny street. I thanked the fellow for being so kind.

After a few language mess-ups the next morning, we got on our train, this time straight to Paris. I rejoiced as best I could about crossing the Alps in broad daylight. At times, the train was about like that darned little old car, barely enough power to get up the hill, but then it'd move through thin white clouds and we'd ooh and ah about the snow-covered mountain peaks and the valleys where snow laid deep, and little towns took on the look of miniature sets from *The Sound of Music.* Man, I couldn't help it! I hummed "The Hills are Alive" two are three times, then after a little while, I asked my wife and daughter to harmonize with me to sing "Edelweiss," but they thought that was stupid and never looked up from scanning a magazine they'd bought in Florence called "Shopping Paris." My wife kept showing me this and showing me that. Son of a gun! That magazine had all the same old junk I could buy for half the price, maybe even less, at Wal-Mart in Alabama. Anyway, I hummed "Edelweiss" in my head and nearly came to tears when I thought about the captain, Maria, and the kids crossing those mountains on foot, maybe, I figured, right up there ten thousand feet in the clouds. It took me a little while to get my head back on right, and then I checked the brochure. It said we'd enter the "Black Forest" around one o'clock and stop at a little old town to change the train's crew. Darn! I remembered that "Black Forest" was a cake I'd eaten in a German restaurant back home; it was so sweet it nearly killed me that night. Heck, my stomach started churning like crazy on that train and I felt like I was going to vomit right there in our compartment. My wife said to take a few deep breaths; the air was thin that high in the Alps. I couldn't help thinking I was in a dream of some sort and couldn't get out, and then the train jumped, started up again. I figured the crew had changed, but would you believe that my whole darn life was dropped into a full-fledged nightmare after just a few minutes more?

My head was back and my eyes were closed, and I think I must have been drooling a little when the door to our compartment flew open. Right there in front of me, my wife, and daughter stood two kids about twenty years old, all decked out in fancy green uniforms, and each wore a cap with a badge on the front. The main one snapped his heels like I remembered in the army, and he said mean-like: "Tickets and passports, please." His eyes were blue daggers that passed from me to my blond wife and black-haired daughter. And let me say this, my daughter's hair is the color mine use to be, as black as coal.

Look Away, Look Away

But anyway...those two young men said to hand them our tickets and passports. I had to fumble through my fanny pack to find everything, then my stomach turned over a couple of times. That green uniform glanced at my daughter's papers, then at my wife's, and finally at mine, and his eyes squinted like a cat that had found a rat. He got mad then and slapped all three tickets in his hand. "You have illegally entered into German territory," he yelled, and I could feel his breath on my face. I think he must have had red onions for lunch, and right then when I glanced at that badge on his cap, it had turned into a darn swastika, as black as I remembered all the way back to World War II. Before I could catch my breath, Hitler snapped his heels again. I figured right off that I could tackle those two rascals and die with honor like an old war hero rather than join up with that long line of sad people with a yellow star sewed on their black coats. I looked at my beautiful wife and beautiful daughter just when they flipped another page in the *Shopping Paris* magazine, then the bigger rascal in front of me laughed: "Just kidding, just kidding; I sell you tickets right now." Huh! It sure wasn't funny, not to me it wasn't.

I recovered from the Black Forest thing at about the same time that old train crossed into France, and the crew changed again. I slept till the train stopped at the station outside of town. In the blur of white heat full of gray dust, we rolled into downtown Paris around five in another little old car about the size of my car's trunk with no air-conditioning, and the driver kept flirting with my daughter. But the rascal did say, in pretty good English, that Paris was in the grip of the worst heat wave in recorded history. Can you believe that? Can you, really?

The hotel room was small, little, really, with a double bed and rollaway with red sheets, and no air-conditioning. *No,* I thought, *this ain't what I thought I'd find in Paris.* Heck, no; I remembered the gilded moldings and marble statues in the brochure my wife and daughter had shown me, and a view of that dang Eiffel Tower straight out the bedroom window, and boy, do you know what else had sold me on that trip: France's National Museum Gustave Moreau... because, can you believe this...Momma's mother's name was Moreau, Clara Moreau, before she married Grampaw Armand, around 1900. Their folks were settlers in Louisiana when France owned it, and I figured the ticket man at the National Museum would give us free passes with our being relatives and all. But heck, I could barely think at all about the museum, it was so darn hot in that stupid little room. My wife sat on the side of the bed and started crying. I'd had several scrapes with women in my lifetime, but a woman crying was one thing that made me fold up like an old washrag, and I remembered that most of the scrapes I'd lost anyway. It was then that I pulled out my almost worn-out hotel registry and found another hotel with air-conditioning, just one block off the Champs-Élysées. *Yes,* I thought, *that's where the darn Lido de Paris is!* In case you're not familiar with Paris, Lido de Paris is the girly show that hadn't missed a night of stimulating show-goers for almost eighty years. But what the heck; there was no way I could suggest we go there; only if my wife or daughter happen to ask for a world-renowned place to visit for fine entertainment. But, darn it, they'd never asked me about anything I wanted to put on the list…in fact, several days back they assured me that I had handled the entire trip better than they expected, especially the luggage and opening and closing my wallet. I guess you know what I'm saying, don't you? Just buttering me up was what they were doing.

Anyway…an hour later, we checked into the Paris de Maison and got a darn smaller room with only two single beds. Right then and there, I thought I'd been tricked by God himself, tricked by this stupid trip and made a fool of. My wife said something like that, but we pushed the two beds together and figured we could sleep crossways. When I found the bathroom, the toilet was hidden between a white-tile shower heavily decorated with black mold and a sink no bigger than my darn gumbo bowl. And you wouldn't believe the toilet…solid copper and striped in green, some as blue as the dome on the Methodist church back home. Standing there, I gagged twice, and I knew that stupid toilet would be what I would remember Paris for. Believe me, that thing made me ever so grateful the United States and Sweet Home Alabama were years behind Paris in what has now become known as "going green" with darn water-saver toilets. But, you know how it is…toilets are a lifesaver sometimes, I guess. Am I right or not?

Sleeping crossways on those single beds wasn't good, not at all, so I got up with a sore hip then took a hot shower that made me feel dirtier because of that black mold. Anyway, I stepped out the hotel's door around eight and heard the yelling and screaming a block away on the Champs-Élysées, the "greatest avenue in Europe," they say. When I got there, fifty thousand screaming people were lined up on the sidewalks, so I decided to cross to the other side. Darn it! Right in the middle of that big old street, the policeman grabbed my arm just when a streak of color whizzed by on four or five bicycles, and he kept yelling to get out the darn way..."Tour de France, Tour de France," was all I understood him say. On the other side, I watched and the crowd went crazy for sure when some odd-ball Spaniard won that stupid race, again, for the fourth straight year, I heard later. I figured it was a good deal bigger thing than the bicycle races like those I'd run on our dirt roads when I was kid. Anyway, I pulled out my flamenco dancer fan and spread it open, figuring there'd be at least a little decent recognition for the fastest Spaniard around. And God forgive me if I'm lying, but I'm not—a full-fledged riot almost blew up, so I folded up my fan, sneaked away, and the fussing went on anyway.

A little ways up was a grove of trees and the great big Arc de Triomphe, where a lot of people stood around cursing, I guess, and griping about losing the bicycle race. You know something—I didn't care one way or the other about who won, and I thought the whole bunch was carrying on too much about a few skinny men in tight pants peddling bicycles all over the darn place. So, I headed into the trees to rest my sore hip, sitting on one of the benches in the shade.

The first bench I came to was a two-seater and pretty much covered over with a fat man eating a croissant with jelly in it. Darn! It made me hungry, but I kept on to the next bunch of benches and found a three- or four-seater with an old woman on one end with a little old French flag in her hand and an old man on the other, slurping up the last drips of ice cream on a stick, so I excused myself and sat in the middle. Boy, let me tell you…in two seconds, I figured the devil must have left the door open because those two were straight from hell. The old lady shot up and tried to stab me with her flag, and the old man, like he was crazy or something, started yelling for a policeman, and I hadn't even said a word, except "excuse me." And sure enough, by the time I got fifteen feet away, the policeman grabbed my arm. I told the rascal I was American, and the big man shook me for a second and said in English about like mine that he'd take me to jail if I didn't stop bothering the old folks; they could settle their own dispute about Tour de France.

I looked down at the sidewalk trying not to step on any cracks, or break my momma's back, and thinking it was time for me to get on home to Alabama, and I limped on through the trees to another bench I could see about forty yards away. Right before I got there, I heard a screech, and a little old monkey in a green suit and red hat jumped from behind one of the trees. And then a man about a hundred years old stepped out, too, dressed just like that monkey. He started turning a handle on a box, and I figured he was what I remembered when I was kid at the county fair back home, what we called an organ grinder, and I had to laugh to myself about that name…but anyway, the man had that monkey tied to the end of a long chain. The face on the old man was something else, completely worn out, with a purple nose and purple-and-red skin that looked like an old leather purse left out in the rain and sun, all cracked and broken. Good gosh a-mighty…what else was going to happen? *And you know*, I kept saying to myself, *you're in Paris, France.* But believe me when I say it...the old man and that monkey made a perfect picture, looked so much alike and even stood on bowlegs about the same. Before I knew it, though, that stupid monkey ran toward me and held out a dirty old tin cup and kept chattering something impossible for me to figure out, so I dropped all my change in the cup. And would you ever guess that stupid monkey jumped straight on my shoulder and started picking in my hair, then he kissed me? The organ grinder jerked the chain, and the monkey grabbed me around the neck, like I was his momma, or something. Then the old man came, scolded that monkey, and got him off me. He said something in French, and I headed farther down to the next bench. I stretched out my legs, trying to rest my hip, and that's when Manny came along.

Well, wouldn't you know it! Finally, somebody with a little sense...yeah, that was Manny. Right off, I knew that boy was happy by his big smile, even though he didn't have any legs at all and was strapped to a dinky, makeshift cart with four roller-skate wheels screwed to its underside. And Manny was his own power. He held a wooden piece with a chalkboard eraser nailed to it in each hand, and that's how he pushed his cart along. Poor guy, he was worn and tattered but a good-looking son of a gun in the face, big arms from all that work of getting himself about on his little old throne, and he was dusty. I was kind of embarrassed for Manny because he had no legs and was so low to the ground, but I figured I'd best not say anything. Manny spoke first, in French, and I held up my hands and smiled: "American," I said, and then he opened up with English-type English and poor fellow, he told me his predicament. His purse had been stolen during the bicycle race and he needed enough cash to get back to London, and he asked if I could spare a few francs. Well, I hadn't been in Paris long enough to get any francs yet and I'd already given that stupid monkey all my change, so I pulled my wallet out of my fanny pack and looked at the only cash I had left, a hundred-dollar bill was all. I cut my eyes to Manny's folded pants and that crazy little cart he was strapped to and thought: *For once I can do something really good for somebody, and I'll be there when it happens.* Manny's face lit up like a Roman candle at Christmas when I handed him that hundred. He grabbed my hand and shook it, and I nearly screamed he squeezed it so hard. That boy turned his little old cart on a dime and slapped those eraser pads to the concrete, and as he shot away, he called out that he'd pray for me and God was going to bless me. I shook my hand to get the blood back in, and you know something? Right away I felt better, and I needed to, because I knew that as best I could recall, I'd thought some pretty ugly thoughts and said a few bad words when nobody was around. I really figured God might be a little angry at this old boy here, but with Manny's help, maybe God would see fit to pass a few blessing my way.

Anyway...the next day we made it to the Louvre, you know...probably the greatest museum in the world, and we found the one-and-only old *Mona Lisa* shielded behind thick Plexiglas and hung thirty feet away from the railing, because a bunch of crazy people had hurled something at it. Then we went to the Eiffel Tower. I figured I'd go as high up that thing as they'd let me, but guess what—they were painting it so we had to look at it from a whole block away. And you know what? We never made it to France's National Museum Gustave Moreau, where I was sure I could have made a blood connection to my great granddaddy, but anyway, I never even got around to mentioning the Lido de Paris. That place wouldn't be up my wife's and daughter's alley one bit, at least I don't think it would have been. But anyway.

By the third day, my hip had gotten used to those stupid beds, and believe me I was glad of that. We packed up our things and headed to the airport, and I was glad of that too, ready to head on home to sweet Alabama. I told my wife and daughter to go on and I'd handle the inspection of our bags for contraband...you know, the stuff you want to bring home without paying taxes on it, or maybe a cheap ashtray or towel with the hotel's name on it that you can show off to your friends at home.

I stood there, waiting. "What?" I asked when the inspector glared at my folded flamenco fan and a banana in my shirt pocket. His face lit up and he motioned with his rubber-gloved hand to another darn man in a blue uniform right next to him. That fellow shook his head, cut his eyes to my face then reached and took my fan. He spread it open and smiled when he saw the flamenco dancer, a good-looking woman. Then that rascal winked at me and grabbed my banana. *Son of a gun,* I thought, and he motioned toward the back with his thumb then took me by the arm. When we rounded the corner, I was almost run over by a speeding electric wheelchair padded in blue leather with a little man dressed sharply like he'd just stepped out of a Sears's catalogue, even had a little red beret on his head. His pants legs were neatly folded in front, and alongside was a fashionably dressed, beautiful woman, laughing and giggling. "Hi, Manny," I said, "how you doin', boy?" He glanced up to me, then at the man holding my arm, shook his head, and sped away. Can you figure that? Just try!

"Must eat," the man said in no uncertain terms and poked me in the chest with my banana.

"But I'm not hungry right now," I told him, "and I need to get on my plane."

"Eat," that rascal demanded right there next to a trash can, then he peeled my banana with those rubber gloves. "US allow no fruit in."

I sighed like the devil when the plane leveled off at thirty-five thousand feet and the movie we'd watched three times on the way over came on again. My wife asked if I'd share my banana and I whispered I'd already eaten it.

"That was awfully greedy of you," she said. I closed my eyes, pretending to doze, so she wouldn't get on me about that stupid banana business.

The hum of those four big old engines started putting everybody to sleep, and the teenager next to me drooled with her head leaning my way, so I placed a napkin over the wet spot on the front of her blouse. She jumped like crazy, said a couple of really dirty words straight in my face, and then threw the napkin at me. The snoring big man in front of me had earlier leaned back his seat and jiggled my orange juice, which was sticky on my bare legs and yellow on the front of my short britches. It just seemed like to me that nobody appreciated kind gestures anymore, not anybody. Darn it!

"What a wonderful ten days. Now aren't you glad we did this?" my wife asked in a whisper.

"Yeah," I said just as she snuggled her head onto my shoulder and closed her eyes. Right past that mean teenager, a really fat woman dressed in a striped dress and with a kerchief on her head tied in a knot under her chin, opened a diaper on a screaming baby kicking like crazy on the drop-down tray. *Good Lord a-mighty,* I thought, and the second time she wiped that baby's butt, I gagged and tasted that stupid banana.

"Well, is 'yeah' all you have to say about it?" my wife whispered again.

"That's about it, I guess."

"Well," she sighed, "I thought we'd plan another adventure to Paris in a couple years." Then she went dead out, and I was glad. I didn't want to talk about our trip to Europe, not just yet, anyway.

I tried and tried, but I couldn't take my eyes off that stinky little baby pressed to the momma's big old breast, and I figured she'd be wiping that baby's bottom again pretty soon. I planned to count and keep track of how many times that baby would poop before we landed in New York.

I ruffled my pillow and closed my eyes. Manny's face and his makeshift pad in the park appeared like an old black-and-white still from *The Grapes of Wrath*, then I saw his face and how he smiled when he grasped that hundred-dollar bill. *He said he'd pray for me and God would bless me. Darn, he didn't pray—I know he didn't, must've forgot or something.*

The lights went out.

"Hummmmm," the engines sang, soft and assuring, taking us home to sweet Alabama.